D0626887

THE INFAMOUS

GOING WILD

CHECK OUT ALL OF FRANKIE'S "MARKS"

Book 1: **STEALING GREENWICH**

THE INFAMOUS
Frankie Lorde

GOING
WILD

BRITTANY GERAGOTELIS

PIXEL✚INK

PIXEL✛INK

Text copyright © 2021 by Brittany Geragotelis

All rights reserved

Pixel+Ink is a division of TGM Development Corp.

Printed and bound in August 2021 at Maple Press, York, PA, U.S.A.

Cover and interior design by Steve Scott

www.pixelandinkbooks.com

Library of Congress Control Number: 2020944065

HC ISBN 978-1-64595-057-8

eBook ISBN 978-1-64595-073-8

First Edition

1 3 5 7 9 10 8 6 4 2

To every kid out there who's ever stood up for someone
who couldn't stand up for themselves.
Frankie would be proud.
And so am I.

THE INFAMOUS
Frankie Lorde

GOING WILD

Entry One

I'm a thief.

No joke.

And not the cute kind of thief that steals a lipstick or toy at the corner store. You know, like *you* might've done that one time on a dare. For me, that's child's play.

Nope. I'm the kind of thief that studies the layout to a billionaire's mansion and then steals his four-million-dollar suit of armor. Or sneaks in through the window of a factory to take a two-pound European white truffle worth over $300,000.

I'm *that* kind of thief.

And so is my dad—

Was.

Is?

Can he still be considered a thief if he's in prison?

Never mind. I suppose that doesn't matter.

What matters is that my dad is Tom Lorde: the most notorious international thief the modern world has ever seen. Before the FBI caught him and threw him behind bars, my dad had pulled over forty jobs, stolen around $57 million, and conned some of the smartest people on the planet out of their hard-earned treasures.

And I, Frankie Lorde, helped him do it.

See, I was his right-hand gal.

His coconspirator.

His partner in crime.

His student.

And now, with Dad locked up, and me on my own, the student has become the teacher.

Sort of.

Because what I've learned these past few months while living my new life is that some things you just don't grow out of. They're a part of you, like having a crooked smile or a cowlick. No matter how many times you try to get rid of it, it always creeps back.

So, yeah.

Like I said before: I'm Frankie Lorde, and I'm a thief.

Entry Two

This is my confession.

Well, not so much a confession. More like a memoir? My government-appointed therapist, Dr. Deerchuck, calls it a *journal*. Which I suppose is accurate, though there's something about that term that makes me all prickly. I think it's because it reminds me of the overly happy girls in commercials who are laughing as they write in their glittery pink diaries about their crushes.

I am so not a pink, glittery kind of girl.

The truth is, the only reason I'm writing in this journal at all is because I was forced to. Dr. Deerchuck swears that the more honest I am about my past, the quicker I can let go of it. AKA, the quicker I can be reformed.

The only thing *I* believe is the sooner I do what she says, the sooner I can let go of *her*.

But back to the journal thing. The problem with her logic in letting go of my past is . . . I'm not sure I *want* to.

See, I don't exactly view my life before getting caught as being, well, *bad*. Sure, Dad and I broke a few (hundred) rules. Took some stuff that didn't exactly belong to us. But because of our lifestyle, we got to travel to incredible places, like Paris, Greece, and India. I got to light a candle at Notre Dame. Touch monuments in the Acropolis. Eat sushi while climbing Mount Fuji.

What other middle schooler can say that?

None that I know, that's for sure.

So, when the courts sent me to live with my closest relative—my dad's younger brother, Uncle Scotty—in the quasi-perfect Greenwich, Connecticut, I sort of freaked.

Greenwich is like *Pleasantville*. Only, with mansions and money. Not exactly my style.

And being stuck here for the foreseeable future felt a little like being locked away myself.

It still does, sometimes.

There *are* a few things that make living here suck a little less, though.

One is my uncle Scotty.

Which is a surprise, because he's a cop.

That's right.

We're *literally* playing Cops and Robbers here.

But for whatever reason, it works for us. We even have fun. Like this morning, for instance.

Over the past few months, we've taken to doing a sort of music roulette in the morning. Whoever gets to the kitchen first chooses whatever song they want to listen to. Then the other picks the next song and so on and so forth. But after a few rounds of listening to some pretty great songs, we switched to choosing awful songs for some reason. Sort of like finding the best of the worst to torture each other with. It had become a

4

game of trying to out-annoy each other, until there was a clear winner.

Which was usually me, since I had a plethora of current cringe-worthy pop music to choose from.

This morning Uncle Scotty was already in the kitchen drinking an espresso when I trudged in, which meant he got first pick.

I yawned as I plopped down into what had become *my* chair.

"Pick your poison, Detective," I said, pulling the container of cereal over to my bowl and pouring until it was full.

"I think today's *my* day, Frankie," Uncle Scotty said, leaning against the counter in the same lazy way my dad always had.

A sudden wave of sadness rushed over me as I thought of him, and I tried to shake it off. It was far too early for nostalgia.

"You say that every morning," I answered, pointing at him with my spoon.

"Today it's true," Uncle Scotty replied.

"Doubt it," I said, my mouth full of crispy cereal. "But go ahead and give it a shot."

He just looked at me and raised a determined eyebrow. "Google, play 'I'm Gonna Be (500 miles).'"

The rhythmic strumming of a guitar filled the room and I immediately felt the urge to start nodding along. This was almost always the case. The songs tricked you by starting out sounding normal. But then once the lyrics came into play, it usually went downhill—fast.

A few chords into this one and I could already tell there was something about it that was off.

Or rather, *awful*.

One thing was sure, Uncle Scotty had definitely brought his A-game this particular morning.

"Oh, yeah!" he said loudly over the beginning of the song. "*When I wake up . . .*"

Then to my surprise, my very professional uncle suddenly leaped from his place at the counter into the middle of the kitchen, and struck a crazy pose while holding a spoon up to his mouth like it was a microphone. When the chorus finally hit, he began to march around me while singing the lyrics at the top of his lungs and wiggling his butt back and forth.

"Oh. My. *God*," I said, momentarily frozen in place. "What is happening?"

This was *not* the uncle Scotty I knew. The uncle Scotty I knew wore a serious expression most of the time, jeans and a button-down shirt all of the time, and a silly side . . . well, none of the time.

Until now. This uncle Scotty was new.

"Say it," he demanded, a smile creeping onto his face.

"No way," I said.

"Say it or I'll keep *singing*," he added, jumping around again. "I might even make it your ringtone."

"Fine!" I said, giving in. "You win!"

"What was that?" Uncle Scotty said, putting his hand to his ear like he hadn't heard me.

"You win!" I yelled, with a little laugh. Then I added, "This round."

"All I heard was that *I win*," he said, picking back up his coffee and smoothing down his hair.

"If I didn't know any better, I'd think you actually *liked* that monstrosity," I said, raising an eyebrow.

He smiled, unashamed. "Correction: I *loved* it."

"But we're choosing awful songs," I said, confused.

"I said *I* loved it," he explained. "I knew you'd hate it. Your generation could never appreciate its greatness."

I shook my head at him. "Who *are* you even?"

"I'm your blood, kiddo," he answered, slightly out of breath. "And this—" he said, motioning to his crazy display of dancing, "—is hereditary."

"What's hereditary?" someone chimed in from behind me. "And what in the name of all things Gucci are you guys listening to?"

I recognized the voice right away and didn't bother turning around. Instead, I grabbed one of the danishes we'd picked up from our favorite yummy bakery in town, Black Forest Pastry Shop, and held it up in the air as an offering.

It quickly disappeared from my hand as my friend Ollie collapsed down into the chair next to me.

Entry Three

"Apparently, questionable taste and bad dancing run in the family," I answered him, taking another bite of cereal. "And you'll have to ask Uncle Scotty about the tunes. He's the one who picked *this* winner."

We both turned to look at Uncle Scotty expectantly.

"Seriously?" Uncle Scotty asked us as we waited for an answer. "'Five Hundred Miles'? The Proclaimers?"

We continued to stare at him blankly.

"The theme song from *Benny & Joon*?" he asked, starting to sound exasperated.

"Are they like, Bonnie and Clyde?" I asked.

"Or Thelma and Louise?" Ollie chimed in, miming driving in a car.

"No," Uncle Scotty said. Then he added, hopefully, "It stars Johnny Depp?"

"This is *Johnny Depp* singing?" Ollie exclaimed, perking up.

This time it was Uncle Scotty's turn to stare at us.

When he finally spoke, it was with zero enthusiasm.

"Words cannot express how disappointed I am right now," Uncle Scotty said, placing his mug in the sink.

"Your punishment will be to watch the movie with me tomorrow night."

"I could get behind some movie-theater popcorn," Ollie said looking at me for confirmation.

I shrugged my shoulders.

"It's not in theaters!" Uncle Scotty bellowed, throwing his arms up in the air. "It's a *classic*."

I leaned toward Ollie. "That's code for *old*."

Ollie grimaced.

"Are we being punished?" Ollie asked Uncle Scotty, confused.

When he caught Uncle Scotty's less-than-thrilled expression at that, he sat up straighter in his seat and swallowed hard.

"No offense, Detective Lorde, but based on this song, I'm not sure we can trust your judgment in movies," Ollie said, choosing his words carefully.

Uncle Scotty let out a loud growl and stalked out of the room.

"I said, 'no offense,'" Ollie mumbled under his breath.

I chuckled.

"What was that all about, anyway?" Ollie asked, nodding his head in the direction of where Uncle Scotty had disappeared to.

"No clue," I said, just as confused by the interaction as he was. "He's been weird this whole morning."

"I like to think that *the Detective* buys these just for

me," he said, using his nickname for Uncle Scotty, picking up another pastry and devouring it in one bite.

"Well, *I* don't eat them," I said, not exactly confirming his theory. "I'm a croissant girl myself."

A large smile spread across his face.

"He likes me! He really likes me!" he exclaimed happily.

"I wouldn't go that far," I responded with a snort.

"Neither would I," Uncle Scotty said in what I could tell was a semiplayful tone, as he stalked back into the room. He was fully ready for work now. Gone was the goofy smile and old college track shirt he'd been wearing. He'd changed into a pair of fitted jeans and a blazer, and plastered on his signature furrowed brow. His hair was a bit longer than one would expect in his line of work, but it was styled, so it still managed to look professional.

If I squinted my eyes real tight, I could almost imagine what Dad would've looked like in his younger days. Handsome, fit, maybe a little intimidating in the right circumstances.

"Why are you looking at me like that?" Uncle Scotty asked as he filled his travel mug with more coffee.

I released my squint and looked away.

"No reason," I said, the image and thought dissolving almost immediately. "Um, don't forget I have my call with Dad tonight at seven p.m."

Uncle Scotty's back was to me, but I could see him pause in the middle of gathering his things for work. It only lasted a second, but it was long enough for me to notice it. "I remember," he said as he finished packing his leather messenger bag.

"We're supposed to talk about when I can go visit," I added, getting up and placing my bowl in the sink.

"Sounds good," he added, swinging around to give me a smile. "Okay, kiddos. Gotta go. People to arrest, cases to solve."

I cocked my head to the side curiously as I watched him cross the room.

"Make good choices today," he added behind his shoulder.

As the door clicked shut, Ollie licked the sugar off his fingers and stood up.

"I still say he likes me," Ollie said to himself. Then he turned to me. "Shall we go?"

"Mmmm," I said, distracted. When Ollie's words finally clicked, I shook my head and fixed my eyes on his. "Yeah. Let me just grab a sweater."

As I got up to retrieve the fuzzy gray oversized cardigan I'd picked out for the day, Ollie followed me.

"Spill," he said, in an almost accusatory tone.

"Huh?" I asked.

"What's going on, Frankie?"

"It's nothing," I said, slipping the sweater on.

"Girl, I *know* you. And I know that look," he said, placing his hands on his hips, wrists facing out. "You might not have noticed, but I'm a *master* of perception."

11

I snorted at that.

"For real!" he insisted. "I can tell something's on your mind."

I rolled my eyes. Ollie insisting he was a master of perception was like a person who knows a simple card trick saying he's a magician.

It was the overstatement of the year, but I was willing to give him the benefit of the doubt.

"Okay," I said, raising my eyebrow at him, challengingly. "Then tell me what's bugging my uncle? If you're such a *master* and all."

Ollie's face scrunched up in confusion. He hadn't been ready for that.

"Uh, he was annoyed that we didn't like his song?" he offered, obviously missing all the clues that Uncle Scotty had unknowingly put out there.

"Well, *yes*," I answered, ushering him to the door. "But what had him running out of here so fast?"

"Work?" Ollie said quickly.

I shut the door behind us, and before we'd even stepped off the porch, I made a sound like a buzzer on a game show.

"Ehhhhh! Thanks for playing, though!" I said, faking enthusiasm before revealing why he was wrong. "First off, my uncle isn't intimidated by *anyone*. Second, the thing that was bothering him had nothing to do with work."

Ollie pulled the hood of his bright red wrap coat over his head and tried to block out the cold air of the morning.

I hadn't noticed it before, but Ollie's outfit looked fairly reminiscent of Little Red Riding Hood. Not that this was exactly surprising for my fashionista friend. Ollie's wardrobe was like a visual journal. He literally wore his heart and mood on his sleeve.

So, if he was channeling little Miss Hood, did that make me the big, bad wolf?

Some might say yes.

I wasn't so sure. Lately I'd been feeling a bit more like a domesticated wolf cub who'd lost her growl than a wild dog on the prowl. That's what happened to animals in captivity. They began to lose their true selves.

For a thief like me or my dad, that would be a fate worse than death.

"Then enlighten me, wise master," Ollie said, pulling me out of my thoughts. "What *is* bugging *the Detective* these days, if it's not work."

Ah, yes, Uncle Scotty. The Lorde that was already housebroken.

"It's got something to do with my dad," I said, dropping the bomb.

Ollie's eyes widened at the mention of my old man.

"You think *the Detective's* worried he's busting out?" he asked, practically salivating at the thought.

I sighed.

Ollie was sort of obsessed with my dad. In fact, it was this same obsession that had allowed him to recognize me on my first day of school just a few months back. He'd been glued to the TV during my dad's trial and had seen right through the mousy make-*under* I'd given myself in an attempt to go unnoticed. It hadn't taken Ollie long to admit that he was a fan—not in the criminal sense—and had dreams of playing Dad in the biopic of Tom Lorde that he swears will be made one day.

I prayed it never did.

"He's not worried about Dad breaking out," I answered Ollie while kicking at a rock. "Though, I'm sure Dad's been working on a plan ever since he got in there."

Ollie's head turned to me like it was on fire.

"Did he tell you that?" he asked excitedly.

"Nah. It's just what we do. Like, I don't need to tell you that I'm already working on some ideas for our next plan," I explained to him simply. Ollie blinked at that like it was news to him, but I continued. "No, it's more like . . . Uncle Scotty doesn't want me to *talk* to my dad or something."

"But why? He seemed pretty cool when you mentioned it before."

"He was definitely *not* cool about it," I said, shaking my head and chuckling to myself. Sometimes I forgot how much the average person missed when it came to body language.

"Okay, so tell me what I missed," Ollie instructed. "I'm ready to learn."

I glanced over at him and could see he was serious. He *wanted* to know about this stuff.

I took a deep breath and began. "Well, first off, Uncle Scotty's whole body tensed up when I mentioned my phone call with Dad tonight," I said, recounting the incident in the kitchen. "Stiffening up or momentarily stopping what you're doing is like, your body's fight-or-flight response. Only, there's one more *F* that's more common: freeze. Uncle Scotty *froze* when I mentioned talking to Dad, so that probably means he's uncomfortable with the idea and doesn't know how to respond."

"Couldn't he have just been distracted?" Ollie asked. "And it was just poor timing on when it kicked in?"

I nodded slowly. "Sure. And if the pause was it, then you might be right," I said. "But it wasn't."

"Oh," Ollie said, frowning. "What else, then?"

"There was his smile when I mentioned the call," I offered.

"I remember that!" Ollie exclaimed proudly.

"And what do you remember about it?" I asked him like a teacher prompting her student.

"It was really big," Ollie said. "I know he likes to act all *grumpy cop*, but I remember thinking that I'm definitely his favorite out of all of your friends."

"Newsflash, Ollie: you're my only friend," I pointed out.

"And let's keep it that way."

"No arguments here," I agreed. "I will, however, have to take issue with your recollection of Uncle Scotty's smile."

"Why?" he asked, surprised.

"Because it was one hundred percent fake," I responded matter-of-factly.

Ollie raised an eyebrow. "How could you tell?"

"It's all in the eyes, my dear friend," I said. "Or rather, *not* in the eyes."

Ollie let out a frustrated sigh. "So, which is it?"

"A real smile puts a crinkle in the corner of your eyes," I revealed. "And Uncle Scotty had no crinkle."

"Maybe he's just worried about getting crow's feet," Ollie suggested as he touched the area near his eyes gently. But after a second, he seemed to abandon that theory. "Okay, so *the Detective's* got a problem with you talking to your dad. What are you going to do about it?"

"Nothing," I said. "*For now.* Until he tells me there's a problem, there *is* no problem. But I'm definitely filing it away."

Entry Four

School had a way of ruining everything.

Case in point: Three weeks ago, classes let out for winter break.

But instead of getting to take a much-needed mental break from everything scholastic, the powers that be at Western Middle School decided to force us all to take on an extracurricular assignment during our vacation.

(Yet another reason I'm convinced Dad had the right idea to keep me out of school all those years.)

In a fit of what could only be described as sheer insanity, we were suddenly required to sign up for community service. More specifically, we had to complete a total of twenty-five hours of volunteer work at one of the local charitable organizations before heading back to school mid-January. There had been a special curated list to choose from, ranging from soup kitchens and hospitals to libraries and shelters.

After discussing our options, Ollie and I decided on two things:

One, that we wanted to volunteer someplace together.

And two, that we needed to find a place that didn't completely suck.

We got both of those with The Farm.

And after having volunteered there for the past three weeks, we could now say that we loved it. Not that we'd ever admit to Western Middle that they'd done anything right.

Nearly fifteen minutes after leaving my house, Ollie and I stopped in front of what looked like an old barn. We'd been volunteering there long enough to know that the inside did not match the outside.

"You ready?" I asked Ollie.

"Sure. If you'll be on litter duty today," he responded hopefully.

I snorted in response as we walked up to the front door.

A tiny bell announced our arrival almost as soon as we'd turned the knob. It seemed unreasonably loud to me and I cringed at the noise it made.

I will never get used to making such an obvious entrance.

"Don't let them escape!" a woman's voice shouted out, pleadingly.

I kicked the door closed just as three cats darted out of hiding to greet us—or more likely, to find their ways to freedom.

"It's us, Kayla!" Ollie yelled out, walking through the room and toward the back.

"Oh, good!" she answered, sounding relieved. "Perfect timing. I could really use some help."

"That's what we're here for," I answered, following behind Ollie.

As we walked farther inside, I glanced around at the two-story open floorplan, which was airy yet cozy. There were exposed beams and distressed wood, as well as decorative square windows along the top that let in plenty of light. Hanging on one of the walls was a large iron art piece that read THE FARM. I remembered the first time Kayla had explained the concept to us. She'd named the place after the old story that some parents gave their kids when their pets had died. "Snowball went to live *on a farm* in the countryside to be with her other doggy friends." "You won't see Lucy for a while because she's living on *the farm* now."

Kayla liked the idea that "The Farm" could actually exist as a place where animals went to live happily ever after—or until they found their forever homes. I had to agree that the concept and name fit perfectly for an animal rescue.

I walked farther into the building and caught sight of another cat out of the corner of my eye, this one stalking us from a beam overhead. I didn't need to be an animal psychic to know what her plan was, and I smiled as I waited for what was coming.

A few seconds later, the white and gray Maine coon wiggled her butt before jumping down from the rafters and right onto Ollie.

"Eeeeeeeowwwww!" he shrieked at an octave I didn't

think he had in him. Having been caught completely off guard, Ollie struggled to remain upright while the cat tried her best to balance on his shoulders.

I cracked up as I sidled up to the two of them and gently retrieved the animal from her new favorite perch.

"Did you see that?" Ollie exclaimed, his chest heaving dramatically. "She's totally trying to kill me! Why doesn't she ever do that to you?"

I shrugged. "She knows she could never sneak up on *me*."

But it was more than that.

Now, I was the first to admit that I wasn't exactly a warm and fuzzies kind of person. But Geronimo had won me over with her completely aloof attitude and mischievous ways.

It was almost like we shared a kinship.

"Geronimo!" I playfully scolded the cat as I scooped her up in my arms and kissed her furry face. "You may have nine lives, but as you know, Ollie does not. Maybe cut him a little slack?"

Ollie scowled at this and mumbled something under his breath as he fell into step behind us—keeping a healthy distance this time, I noticed.

"Hey there, Tiny," I said, leaning down to tousle a two-and-a-half-foot-tall goldendoodle's mop of curly hair before passing into the back where Kayla was.

The rear section of the barn was a different space entirely from what was up front. It reminded me a little like the description of the worst haircut known to mankind: business in the front, party in the back.

The analogy worked because the back of the barn was sectioned off specifically for the rescue animals.

Now, if you were picturing a room like the ones in those really sad animal abuse commercials, don't. First off, it'll make you cry. And then you'll be reading my journal and crying, and people will think you're reading *The Notebook* or something. And that would just be embarrassing—for *you*.

Second, you would be wrong in your assumption.

The reality is, The Farm was nicer than I'd expected a rescue could be. But this *was* Greenwich, so there were certain expectations people had. The town simply wouldn't accept a run-down, dirty-looking business in their clean, sparkly community . . . even if it *was* just a shelter for animals.

With that said, it was really Kayla who insisted the animals in her charge not go from one crappy situation to another. She cared more about them than that.

So much so that she'd given up her cushy pet vet job to open The Farm.

It was just who she was. Nothing was too good for the animals who ended up in her care.

In terms of living conditions, this meant roomy glass cubicles lining the walls to allow each dog their own space to move around comfortably and uncaged. For the animals who were more social, or the ones that arrived with siblings, connecting suites allowed for co-mingling and frequent cuddling.

Above the K-9 units were where the cats were kept in what Kayla aptly called the purr-fect penthouses. Also made of glass, each animal's abode was expansive and equipped with everything the felines needed. For the more playful residents, there were scratching posts, toys, and lounging perches set up all around the room to give the cats plenty of real estate to explore.

I'd taken to calling the animal area the inner sanctum. Because that was what it had become to me: my home away from home.

"Over here!" Kayla called out. She must've heard our shuffling feet because she'd said it even before she could see us.

I carefully placed Geronimo down on the ground and followed Kayla's voice to where she was kneeling next to a big brown box.

"Well, what do we have here?" Ollie asked as he appeared beside me, a big grin on his face.

"We need to get this little guy up and into his new cage," Kayla said.

And then she began to pull out a creature bigger than all of us.

"Holy—*snake*!" Ollie screamed in surprise, and jumped behind me as if I was going to protect him.

I rolled my eyes and scooted forward to crouch down next to Kayla.

My experience with pets may have been limited, but still, I wasn't what you would call squeamish around them. After all, I'd run into my fair share of odd pets while breaking in to places over the years. Rich people collected the strangest stuff. Even animals.

"What do you need me to do?" I asked.

"I'll grab its head and upper body," she said, already switching up her grip on the reptile. "You grab the lower half."

"You got it," I said, moving to do what she asked.

On the count of three, we both stood up, the animal's leathery body feeling like one giant muscle in my hands.

I'd never held a snake before.

It was surprisingly exhilarating.

Ollie did *not* feel the same way.

"You're . . . *touching it?*" Ollie asked from the spot he'd retreated to all the way across the room. He shuddered dramatically.

Straining a bit under the snake's weight, I gritted my teeth. "Is there another way you think we should do this, Ollie? Levitation maybe?" I said. "Or hey, here's a thought . . . you could *help*."

Ollie's face drained of color.

"Nope, looks like you've got it," he said quickly, stepping back once more to put even greater distance between us.

"I already prepped his new home," Kayla said, moving on. "Had to use one of our largest fish tanks."

Taking coordinated steps, we walked over to the empty tank and slowly lowered the snake into it. Once he was inside checking out his new digs, I turned back to Kayla.

"What *is* he?" I asked, placing my fingertips on the outside of the glass next to his face, my way of saying hi. His tongue darted out at me and I imagined what it might feel like to have its breath on my skin.

"A boa constrictor," Kayla said, walking over to the sink and washing her hands.

"I didn't know we had boas in Connecticut," I said.

"We don't," Kayla said. "Not naturally, at least."

Ollie still hadn't moved any farther into the room, and his usually caramel-colored skin had gone white since seeing what was in the box. I decided not to torture him anymore and placed the cover on top, latching the two sides loudly to show him it was secure.

"So, where'd he come from then?" I asked, turning back to Kayla.

"Good question," she responded thoughtfully.

Then, a shadow crossed over her face. It was such an odd reaction coming from her, that it immediately piqued my interest.

Since day one, Kayla had reminded me of a Disney princess. From the melodic singsongyness of her voice to her beautiful pale skin and dark hair, she could've been one of Walt's muses.

She said things like, "Oh my goodness," and talked to

the animals like they talked back to her. She was sweetness and light all wrapped up with a bright, colorful bow, and despite my general thinking that no one was *that* nice, I'd come to believe she was.

But the frown she was currently wearing? This was a side of her I'd never seen before. In fact, I didn't think her face could even move that way.

"You have a theory though, don't you?" I asked her, finishing her thought from before.

Her mouth fell into a surprised O shape, revealing instantly that I was right.

"Well, I don't really like spreading rumors," Kayla's honeyed voice sounded reluctant. "And you two are still so young. . . ."

I could tell she needed a little coaxing, so I complied.

"We won't say anything," I promised.

Kayla gave me a look filled with hesitation. Then everything in her seemed to relax along with the gentle sigh she let out.

"I suppose it's not a rumor if it's true," she said finally, giving in. "Besides, you are supposed to be learning about this business. Even the not-so-fun stuff."

I nodded to let her know it was okay to spill.

Turning away from me, she began to walk around the inner sanctum, picking things up and placing them in their designated spots. Then she handed me and Ollie gloves, plastic bags, and scoopers, and directed us toward the purr-fect penthouses.

"We can talk while we work." She said it so sweetly that I almost forgot she was asking me to pick up poop.

Regardless, Ollie and I let the cats loose so we could clean their houses. Once we'd started working, Kayla began to talk.

"As you guessed, Frankie, boa constrictors aren't from around here," Kayla said as she portioned out lunch for each of the dogs into their designated bowls. "Home for them is actually in Mexico and tropical Central and South America."

"How did they get here then?" Ollie chimed in. Then his face dropped. "Please tell me it wasn't a Snake-nado situation. I couldn't even—can you imagine if it began raining *reptiles*? Nope. No. *No thank you*."

I glared at Ollie, hoping he'd quit babbling, but Kayla just chuckled.

"No, Ollie. Their migration was *not* an act of nature," Kayla said, calming his fears. "It was an act of *man*."

"Meaning . . . ," I said, though I thought I already knew.

"Meaning, some not-so-bright people brought them here."

"Why would they *do* that?" Ollie asked, astonished by the thought.

"People wanted them as pets," Kayla answered.

"Again, *why* exactly?" Ollie asked, making a face.

"It's the whole X *factor*," Kayla explained. "As in, exotic. They think it makes them cool to have something that the average person doesn't. Never underestimate the power of exclusivity among those who can afford it."

No one knew that better than me. If my past had taught me anything it was that rich people loved having things others didn't—no matter how stupid it was. Money, clothes, houses, cars . . . you name it, they wanted it. In fact, the most appealing words to a wealthy person seemed to be "rare," "uncommon," and "one-of-a-kind." Oftentimes, they didn't even *truly* want whatever the object was; it was simply that they didn't want anyone else to have it.

"Once the boas were trafficked into the country to become pets for the elite, it didn't take long for the owners to realize they'd gotten themselves in over their heads. Most don't realize how big they can get, how much the reptiles eat, and how dangerous they can be. So, when they did, they'd dispose of them. One of the ways they did this was by simply setting them free. The other was by killing them."

"I may not be a fan of snakes," Ollie said, glancing over at the boa that Kayla and I had just caged. "But just cutting it loose so it can slither into my house at night and eat my baby cousin? Uh-uh, no way. Unacceptable."

"I agree," Kayla said. "And not just because one of these *could* kill a small child. But two million of them later, we suddenly have a snake problem here in the US. And places like The Farm are asked to take them in."

"Does that happen a lot?" I asked Kayla. "You getting stuck taking care of wild animals I mean?"

She paused. "Not really. But only because I usually say no," she explained. "I *do* get more inquiries than you'd think, though. And to be honest, sometimes I wish I could—who *wouldn't* want to see a white Bengal tiger up close and personal, am I right?"

"Um," Ollie said as he raised his hand slowly.

"Well, for *me* it would be like crossing something off my bucket list," Kayla continued. "But it wouldn't be right. The exotic pet world is a whole different animal completely—pardon the pun. And while a few of my classes in vet school delved into that world, it wasn't nearly enough for me to know what I'd be doing. And besides that, there has to be special housing, it's super expensive to feed them, and the danger factor is off the charts. A big cat wouldn't hesitate to rip your arm off in less than three seconds if given the chance."

"I believe it," Ollie said, narrowing his eyes at Geronimo, who'd wandered into the room while we'd been talking. "Cats definitely can't be trusted."

"You were asked to take care of a tiger?" I asked, ignoring Ollie's comment. "Isn't that sort of crazy? Like, who owns a tiger . . . in *Connecticut*?"

"It's bonkers," Kayla responded. "And yet, it happens. Quite a bit lately, too."

My interest was piqued. "What do you mean?" I asked, the familiar feeling of excitement growing inside my stomach.

Kayla stopped what she was doing and looked around

the inner sanctum as if to make sure we were the only ones there. Which, of course, we were. The secretive nature of this made me almost giddy with anticipation.

"A few months ago, someone from the FBI reached out to me because they'd came across a four-hundred-pound Bengal tiger when they raided someone's home here in Greenwich," Kayla said quietly, her face fully animated as she revealed the information. "Apparently this super wealthy guy had been keeping the tiger as a pet on his estate. But since he was being charged with, like, a dozen crimes, almost everything on his property was being seized and they needed someone to take in the animal."

I swallowed hard as something about her story sounded familiar.

"I told them I couldn't accept the animal—I don't have the space or right enclosures, not to mention the training needed—but ended up connecting them with an exotic big cat rescue not too far from here," Kayla said. "The agents wouldn't give me a ton of details but from what I gathered, the cat had actually lived a pretty good life on the estate. He'd been well fed, was in good shape, and had quite a bit of land to roam on. But still . . . it's a *wild tiger* who was being held in captivity. And the guy was a crook. So, it probably all worked out for the best."

Halfway through her story, Ollie and I had slowly turned to glance at each other. I could see the look of horror and disbelief on his face and was pretty sure that mine mirrored his. Without saying anything, I knew we were both thinking the same thing.

"Huh," I said coolly, as if I didn't really care about any of it. Then I asked the question that made the mounting sickness begin to rise in my belly. "Whose tiger was it?"

The smile broke out over Kayla's face. "That's the best part," she said. "It was *Christian Miles's*."

Entry Five

It was like all the wind had been knocked out of my chest.

Christian Miles?

The same Christian Miles that Ollie and I had plotted against and stolen a fair portion of his fortune from, in order to help the people he'd treated badly, all while party-crashing one of his galas a few months ago?

That guy?

The thought almost made me heave.

Not because I felt guilty for being responsible for him being arrested in the first place—that was a fact I was actually rather proud of.

As far as I was concerned, he'd made his billion-dollar jail-cell bed and now he deserved to lay in it.

The part I felt bad about was that there was an animal out there without a home or someone to care for it . . . because of *me*. And the truth was, of all the possible downsides I'd weighed before deciding whether to go after Miles, this hadn't even made the list.

Still, an innocent animal being harmed in the process of me carrying out a job? That wasn't okay. I might be a thief, but I *do* have a strict code of ethics I live by. And it was very clear on things like this.

I let out the breath I'd been holding in and closed my eyes tightly.

I knew what I had to do.

"What happened to the tiger?" I asked, my back still to Kayla and Ollie.

Somehow I had to make it right.

"Like I said, I put them in touch with the exotic animal rescue just out of town," Kayla said. "It has such a cute name: Born to Be Wild. I met one of the gals who works there, Jessica, at an animal rescue conference in Miami a few years back. She was so sweet, and I remember being jealous that she got to work with the big cats every day."

I filed away the rescue's name in my memory, and vowed to check in on the tiger as soon as I could. I needed to know it was okay. That I hadn't completely ruined the tiger's life.

"How did the billionaire guy get the tiger in the first place?" I asked, needing to know more. "I'm assuming he couldn't just go to his local pet shop."

"No," Kayla answered, laughing. "Definitely not. He probably bought it in an auction? Or more likely, through an exotic animal broker. Since it's technically illegal to own a level one wild animal here in Connecticut, people have to keep things like that on the down-low."

"So, make the broker take the tiger back," Ollie said, shrugging.

"Wish it were that easy," Kayla said. "Then again, if we knew who the brokers were, we might actually be able to make them pay for what they're doing. Take down the broker, and you stop the smuggling of the animals in the first place, ending the abuse of these animals completely."

Something inside me clicked.

"So, really, the bad guys are these brokers?" I asked. "Stop the supply and there is no demand."

"In theory," Kayla said. "But I'm no expert in this field, and don't want to presume I have all the answers. I'm sure it's much more complicated than that."

I nodded as she talked, but I was already ten steps ahead.

"You think the brokers live here? In Greenwich?" I asked.

Kayla seemed to hesitate before answering.

"Obviously this stays between us—and I have no proof—but yeah, I think they're in the area," she said finally.

"Huh," I said, thinking about this. "And you don't have any guesses who it could be?"

Kayla looked at me sideways as she continued to move around the room.

"What's with the sudden interest in the exotic?" she asked me. Her tone wasn't accusatory, more curious.

I needed to tread lightly now. Too much prying would ensure she'd remember this conversation later. And depending on where things went from here, I might not want her to remember this at all.

I shrugged. "Ollie and I have to do research projects

on a topic of interest within the area we're volunteering in," I said, thinking quickly. "I haven't chosen mine yet and, well . . . you've kind of *inspired* me."

The lie came out easily.

I'd had enough practice over the years that they usually did.

Ollie, however, had not.

"I'm doing mine on why dogs are superior to cats!" he yelled out suddenly, even though we hadn't asked. When we both looked over at him, surprised by his outburst, his cheeks glowed red. "Just in case . . . you know . . . you wanted to know."

Plastering a smile on my face, I turned to look at Kayla to see if she was buying any of it. Then I held my breath as I waited for her to respond.

Luckily, she was more trusting than I was.

"Great topics," she said to us, playing along with the absurdity of Ollie's outburst.

I let a beat go by before continuing.

"I just wish we knew who the brokers could be," I said slowly. "It'd be a really great source . . . for my assignment."

Kayla opened the door to the back of the barn, which led to a fenced-in area outside where the dogs and cats could roam around. The ground had been covered with fake grass to protect the animal's sensitive paws and to give them the illusion that they had a nice outdoorsy area to play in. Unfortunately, the space was only about seven by ten feet.

Meaning: not very big.

Kayla had dreams of building a whole fresh air play area out there, complete with bridges, a pond, splash pad, hills, and toys galore. One of the walls in her tiny office had sketches and ideas taped all over it. It was like her real life Pinterest board.

She'd admitted to us that the only thing keeping her from doing it right now was money. As in, she didn't have enough of it. The rescue ran on donations, and in a good year, the money covered all The Farm's expenses.

Needless to say, there was never any extra cash lying around to put toward the animal play yard.

"Sorry, Frankie," Kayla said, seeming like she meant it. "You know what I know now. Wish I could be more help."

I shook my head. "No, this has been super helpful already, Kayla," I said, the beginning of a plan forming. "Really. You have no idea."

Kayla seemed to perk up at this.

Geronimo sauntered in between us then and rubbed up against my leg, purring loudly.

"Hi, girl," I said, leaning down to twirl her tail around my fingers playfully.

Kayla watched us with a smile.

"You know," she said, placing her hands on her hips and peering at me. "You're really great with Geronimo. And you can tell she loves you, too."

"She's a cool cat," I nodded, snapping my fingers so

the furry feline would jump up onto the closest cat tower. When she obediently complied, I scratched behind her ears and then grinned as she stuck her butt straight up into the air with glee.

"Have you ever thought of taking on a rescue, Frankie?" Kayla asked.

The question caught me off guard.

I didn't think I came off as someone who could be trusted to keep a pet alive, but I appreciated that Kayla thought so. Still, I immediately began shaking my head.

"Nah," I answered, hoping it was enough.

It wasn't.

"But you would make such a great cat parent!" Kayla continued pushing. "Especially to Geronimo here. You two have similar personalities, you know. You're both sneaky and adventurous. You're skeptical of people at first, but once you decide you can trust them, you're loyal to the end."

I was kind of shocked by how accurate her description of me was and wondered if maybe I'd underestimated her all this time.

"I appreciate the vote of confidence, Kayla, really. But trust me, I'm not your girl," I said convincingly.

So then why did it feel so much like a lie when I fully believed what I was saying?

Kayla blinked. "Huh. Okay," she said, taking in the resolve on my face. She threw her hands in the air in defeat. "That's so weird. Maybe my radar is wonky today.

I'm usually such a great judge of pet parents. But if you're not a cat person, then you're not a cat person. . . ."

"Sorry," I said, not knowing what else to say. "Besides, my uncle already forbid me to bring home any strays. I guess that's what regular kids do."

"Now *that* I believe," Kayla said with a laugh.

It was my turn to be surprised.

"You know my uncle?" I asked.

"Of course," she said with a twinkle in her eye. "Unfortunately, there are plenty of criminals out there who own pets."

I was confused by her explanation at first, but finally got what she was saying.

"Ahhhh," I said. "And when the criminals go away, the animals end up here."

"Bingo," Kayla said, placing her finger on the tip of her nose. "Your uncle has been to The Farm plenty of times over the years. I was always trying to convince him to get a dog, but he claims he doesn't have the time to take care of one. Whether he's lying to me or to himself, I'm not sure. But I can tell he's lonely. I'd bet money that deep down he just wants someone to come home to at the end of the day."

Then she flashed me a big smile.

"I suppose that person is you now!" she said happily, like it all worked out in the end.

I supposed it was.

Even though we didn't mind being a part of a pack,

the Lordes—at their core—were lone wolves. Uncle Scotty was no exception.

Although, I'd admit that I think he'd gotten used to having me around—maybe even enjoyed having me there most of the time—it's not like it was the ideal living situation for any of us.

That would be Dad getting out of prison and us going on our merry way, and Uncle Scotty having his bachelor pad back.

I planned to talk to Dad about all this when I finally got to see him.

Which hopefully would be soon.

Entry Six

"I can't believe this is finally happening!"

As soon as I'd told Ollie all about my conversation with my dad, he'd started dancing around me in what was his version of an end zone dance after a touchdown.

"You act like it's happening to you!" I exclaimed, laughing and raising an eyebrow.

"It sort of is," he said, his eyes twinkling.

"What does me visiting my dad for the first time since he was arrested, have to do with you?"

"Um, because I finally get to meet the most notorious thief in the world?" said Ollie, like it was obvious. "I mean, don't get me wrong—you're good, but he's a *god*."

I cocked my head to the side sympathetically.

"Sorry, Ollie," I said gently. "It's sort of a family-members-only kind of visit. I think even *I* might've been lucky to get to go—and I'm his daughter! Seems like they're keeping his visitor's list kind of light these days. Mainly just to his lawyers."

Ollie's face scrunched up. I couldn't tell what he was thinking, and with all my knowledge on reading people, that wasn't a good sign. I knew it was Ollie's dream to meet my dad. For some reason he idolized him. And I didn't want him to think that I was trying to take that chance away from him.

When I promised something, I kept my promise.

But it had been months since I'd seen my dad, and I really needed some one-on-one daddy/daughter time. How was I supposed to explain that to someone who *didn't* have a dad that was currently locked away in prison?

"You understand, right?" I asked, not wanting to let down the only friend I had around here.

Ollie looked over at me for a few seconds and then rolled his eyes before bumping his hip into mine.

"Of *course* I understand, F," he said. "But next time, I'm going. I don't care if we have to say I'm your brother. I'll be your brother from another mother. As Francis Ford Coppola is my witness, I *will* meet the infamous Tom Lorde."

I couldn't help but laugh.

"Deal," I promised as we continued on our way.

After a few steps in silence, Ollie cleared his throat.

"So . . . what are you going to say to him?" he asked. "I mean, there's so much to catch him up on—me, for instance—and talking face-to-face is a whole different thing. . . ."

He was right. And it was a good question. One that I'd been thinking about forever now. And one that I still didn't have the answer to.

"Figured I'd just wing it," I said, not exactly lying. I didn't bother going into everything else I was thinking.

I was sure Ollie didn't *really* want to hear my weirdo thought process, and I didn't really want to get into it. "I mean, it's my *dad*. We never had trouble talking before, I doubt it'll be hard now. I'll just talk to him about, I don't know, *whatever. . . .*"

Ollie looked doubtful. "Yeah, but you don't think things will be different now that he's been in the big house?"

"The big house?" I asked, my eyebrow raised. "What era are we in?"

"You know what I mean," he said, brushing off my comment. "And stop avoiding my questions."

"I'm not avoiding them," I said uncomfortably.

But I was.

I let out a big breath.

"Look, of *course* things will be different. Just the fact that I haven't seen him in so long is different," I said carefully. "And I'm not dumb. I've seen prison shows. I know it's not a trip to Disneyland in there. But it's *my dad*. No matter what happens, he'll always be the person who knows me best. He'll always be my best friend."

I said the last part quietly. Not because I was embarrassed that my dad was my best friend. I'd be proud to say that to anyone. He's a cool dude. And I was pretty confident that when we were there in front of each other, it would be like we'd never been apart.

No, the thing that was making me all weird was that I was . . . *conflicted*.

I'd suddenly realized that my dad wasn't my *only* friend anymore.

Because now I had Ollie to lean on.

And I was choosing my own marks, coming up with my own heist plans, *and* training a mentee.

All the things Dad used to do for me.

And that fact made me feel like I was leaving him behind in some way.

Maybe even leaving the old me behind too.

That thought scared me more than anything else. The fact that I was becoming someone I didn't quite recognize.

"Okay," Ollie said quietly, realizing I was having a moment—and thankfully he let me have it. After a few more beats to wrap up my thoughts, he spun around to face me in the middle of the sidewalk.

I stopped, surprised.

"There's something else we need to address," he said, his expression serious.

"What?" I asked, no idea what he was about to say.

After another uncomfortably long pause, he said, "You mention Disneyland a lot. Should I be worried your heart isn't made of stone after all?"

I hit him on the arm and started walking again.

"You're such a jerk," I said. "I thought you were going to say something serious."

"It *is* serious," he insisted, eyes wide. "You liking

Disneyland is just . . . it's like Marilyn Manson liking Britney Spears's music. It's not on-brand."

"I can like Disney," I said almost defensively.

"I don't know if you can," Ollie argued. "Not without upsetting the universe."

"My dad and I have been to every country that Disney has a theme park in," I said, crossing my arms. "It's a sacred place to us. It's the only spot we've never stolen from."

"Now *that's* intriguing," Ollie said, tapping his finger to his mouth and looking off into the distance. "Why?"

I didn't have to think about my answer. "It's the happiest place on Earth," I said. "You don't steal from the happiest place on Earth."

"But you can steal anywhere else?" Ollie asked, sarcastically.

"Not everywhere. There are exceptions," I said. "Believe it or not, we have a strict code we live by."

"There's an official thieves code?" Ollie asked, amazed.

"Of course not," I said, with a wave of my hand. "And I can't speak for all other con men. But Dad and I have a code."

Ollie gave me a look like he didn't believe me.

"There's a fine line between doing bad things and being a *bad guy*. Our code keeps us in that big, beautiful gray area," I explained.

Ollie shook his head. "Whatever you say," he uttered. "I still don't get the Disney thing."

"You don't have to. It's *our* thing anyway. We don't expect anyone else to understand," I answered, slightly annoyed. "New subject, please."

"Okay," Ollie agreed, giving in to my demand. "Let's talk about what happened between you and Kayla at The Farm."

I blinked, lost to the abrupt topic change.

"What are you talking about?" I asked, confused.

"I was heading back inside and caught the end of your conversation," he said plainly.

"You mean you *eavesdropped* on our conversation," I said, crossing my arms.

"Potato, potato," he said, refusing to feel bad about it. "Okay, so what was going on?"

I shrugged. "She just asked if I wanted to adopt Geronimo. You know, since we get along and all."

"Oh, no."

The terrified look on Ollie's face was priceless.

"Don't worry," I added. "I said no."

Ollie let out a breath loudly.

"Not that I want you to bring that bonkers cat home—I know she's plotting to kill me—but why did you say no? You guys are like, homies."

I shrugged again.

"I'm not an animal person," I said, just like I had explained to Kayla.

44

"I don't believe you," he said. "I've seen you with the animals at The Farm, and you're great with them. Way more comfortable than I am."

"That doesn't take much," I joked.

"That might be true, but still, how can you say you're not an animal person?" he asked. "What's the real reason you won't take her?"

"Sheesh, what is this? Interrogate Frankie day?" I asked squirming under his attention.

"If it is, I'm not doing a great job, because you're still not spilling," he said, placing his hand on his hip.

Ugh. He wasn't going to let this go, was he?

"Fine," I said, giving in. "I don't want to take Geronimo because . . . I've never had a pet before."

Ollie's jaw dropped.

"Never?!"

"Hello? We were traveling practically my whole life," I said. "When did I have time to pick up a pet?"

Or set down any kind of roots for that matter.

"It would've made it impossible for us to move around all the time with a dog in tow."

"Well, okay, that makes sense," Ollie muttered. "But now you live *here*. And no more traveling. You can get a cat if you want. It's not like you're going anywhere."

Something about his statement made me frown.

I live here now.

I'm not going anywhere.

That couldn't be right.

Sure, I was staying with Uncle Scotty, and had been enrolled in school and everything, but it's not like Greenwich was my *home*.

Home was with Dad.

Uncle Scotty's place was like . . . a family vacation. A layover before moving on to our next destination.

Eventually, I'd go back to my normal life. Whenever Dad got out and all.

Which Dad and I would hopefully discuss when I saw him.

"Let's just accept the fact that for now, Frankie Lorde doesn't do pets," I said with a playful edge to my voice.

"Okay, F," he said. "Whatever you say."

Was that judgment in his tone or was I just imagining it?

"Besides, how am I supposed to pull off another con if I have to be home to feed the cat?" I challenged. "Unless *you* want to leave in the middle of a break-in to go and take care of Geronimo?"

Ollie was already shaking his head.

"Point taken," he said bluntly. "Nix the cat."

"Thought so," I said, a triumphant smile creeping onto my face.

"Speaking of cons," Ollie said slowly. "I could've sworn I saw a plan forming in your head yesterday."

"Maybe," I answered, cryptically. Then I gritted my teeth. "I'm not psyched that the tiger was caught in the middle of all this. I still think that Christian deserved to go down, but I don't feel great about having left collateral damage in our wake. My gut says we need to make it right."

"Not that I disagree," Ollie started carefully. "But who exactly will we be going after if Christian's already in jail?"

I chewed on my lower lip. "I'm not sure yet," I admitted. "But maybe my dad will have a few ideas. . . ."

Entry Seven

The metal gate clanked shut behind me, the sound echoing loudly in my ears.

You're trapped, it seemed to say.

My armpits and palms began to sweat and my heart started to race at an unnatural speed. I wondered if it was possible for somebody my age to have a heart attack. Surely I wouldn't be the first one.

Ironic though, if I died inside prison—but not as an inmate.

"Don't bother bringing anything in with you," a guard grumbled as soon as I'd walked into the visitor's entrance. "It'll either get stolen or confiscated."

He didn't smile at me.

Not once.

Then again, I probably wouldn't have noticed if he had. I'd been so programmed not to look cops in the eye, on account of being a thief myself, that it came naturally now just to avoid them.

"Don't worry, sugar," said a girl standing beside me as we shuffled through one of the gates.

She was around seventeen, and was wearing cut-off shorts and an old, faded camp T-shirt that seemed like the real deal—not the kind of trendy top that was already distressed when you bought it at the mall. Her hair looked like it hadn't been brushed in a while, and she was wearing bright red lipstick that extended just beyond the natural border of her lips, giving the illusion that they were fuller than they were. The thick, black eyeliner streaking across her top and bottom lids, practically made her eyes disappear completely.

"It's not as bad as it looks," the girl added, taking my silence for fear.

But it was more like . . . sympathy.

I studied the stained floors as we followed the guard in a makeshift line down the hallway to the visitor's room. Did my dad have to clean these floors? Did he have to use a toothbrush and scrub inch by inch like in the movies, or was that all just for dramatic effect? How many prisoners had walked this very same floor while doing penance for their crimes?

Prisoners.

That's what Dad was here.

A *prisoner*.

He wasn't my dad.

He wasn't Tom Lorde, international thief.

He was a *prisoner of the United States*.

I shook the thought out of my head.

No, he'd always be my dad, ahead of everything else.

At least I hoped.

"Sit at the table that matches the number you were given during check-in, and then hang tight," the guard said. "We'll escort the inmates to your tables when we're ready. A reminder of the rules: you may kiss, hug, or shake the hand of an inmate at the beginning of the visit and at the end of the visit. Besides those two specified times, no touching will be permitted. Do not give the inmate any contraband unless it has been approved of ahead of time. Do not rearrange the chairs. Do not talk too loudly, be disruptive, or use profane language."

I followed the guard's instructions, finding the table marked 7, and sitting down on the hard, faded red chair that was there. Almost immediately, I reached for my phone for something to do, but then remembered that I'd had to leave it with Uncle Scotty at the visitor's entrance.

With nothing else to do, I had to just sit there in silence.

Now I was sort of regretting letting Scotty wait in the lobby while I went in.

"If it's okay with you, I'm not going to go in today, Frankie," Uncle Scotty had said to me on the drive to the prison. "I think today needs to be about you and your father."

I had cocked my head to the side in surprise. I'd been sure he'd insist on going in with me—not just because I was still considered young by most standards, but because I figured he'd want to hear what we talked about. I mean, most adults were varying degrees of nosey. And while Uncle Scotty had never really struck me as the type to monitor social media or follow my every move, he was a cop. Gathering information was what he did.

"Look, I get that you've waited for months for your dad to be transferred to a closer *facility* so you could finally see him again," he explained when he saw my face.

Sidenote: Uncle Scotty always said *facility* instead of *prison* when he was talking about my dad. I'm not sure if he thought he was protecting me from the image that the *p* word conjured up, or if he himself didn't want to think of his brother in a place like that.

Maybe it was a bit of both.

"I gather you two have a lot to catch up on and you don't need me around to do it," he said matter-of-factly. "So, unless you're scared and *want* me there with you, I'll just hang back and give you guys your space. Besides, now that my brother's in the area, I can visit him another time on my own."

And that was the moment I realized I kind of loved my uncle Scotty.

He wasn't my dad—no one could be—but he was the closest thing I had now, and I felt pretty lucky.

I don't know another grown-up who would've had the same attitude about the chaos of my life.

And I was so appreciative for the space and trust he was giving me.

Because there were things I wanted to talk to dad about that I just couldn't say in front of Uncle Scotty.

Not because it was about him or anything.

More like, I wanted to talk to Dad about what I'd been up to since he'd been gone. And if I was honest about all of that in front of Uncle Scotty . . . well, let's face it, he might just have to arrest me.

The only door to the room swung open, creaking loudly as if to announce our visitors. My stomach started to do flip-flops as I watched the men shuffle into the room, arms and legs shackled with chains to keep the rest of us safe.

As if I needed to be protected from my dad.

The idea was so preposterous that I almost started to laugh, but then I remembered where I was and clamped my mouth shut.

Man after man entered. They were all different races and shapes, but wore identical outfits, which made your eyes play tricks on you as you tried to pick out your person.

Not Dad.

Not Dad.

Not Dad.

Then, a man with blondish hair and a tall but lean frame walked in. All the other inmates were different variations of pissed, angry, depressed, or tired. This guy was grinning ear to ear.

A guard followed behind him as he made his way over to my table and sat down. Then the guard retreated to a nearby corner and started scanning the room.

Finally, I focused my eyes on the man in front of me.

"Hey, Frankie," he said softly.

"Hi, Dad."

Entry Eight

Nothing could've prepared me for this moment.

Without thinking, I moved toward my dad to give him a hug.

I saw his eyes flicker quickly over to the guard, and I froze halfway across the table.

"Oh," I said, thinking maybe I had broken a rule.

When were we allowed to hug again?

"No. You're fine," Dad said, smiling at me. "Forget them. Come here."

I let out the breath I'd been holding in and let him envelop me in a hug.

He still smelled like himself. There were new fragrances on him too, but it was him. I hadn't thought about how his personal products must've lent to his unique scent. And likely, he couldn't be picky about his toiletries in here. It was probably all generic brands that the government got for next to nothing.

I'd have to remember to send him his favorite deodorant and shampoo. It might make him feel more at home.

Or he could trade it for other contraband. It didn't much matter to me.

Whatever helped him survive in here.

All I *really* cared about was the fact that he still smelled like himself and that gave me hope that other things about him hadn't changed too much either.

"God, it's good to see you," Dad said, studying my face.

I started to shy away, embarrassed by the scrutiny, but then it dawned on me that he might really *need* this. It had been so long since we'd seen each other and even *my* memory was starting to forget some of the details of his face.

And he didn't have anything to remind him of what I looked like—from the beginning, he'd told me not to send pictures of myself.

"Being the proud dad I am, I'd want to put them up in my cell," he'd explained in a letter. "But I don't really want anyone prying into my personal business, if you get what I mean."

I did. And that was fine. I didn't want them to either.

"Your bangs!" Dad said, reaching out to feel my shorn locks.

A clanging sound immediately rang out across the room. We turned in its direction.

"No contact!" the guard warned loudly, gripping his baton tightly

"Sorry," I said nervously.

My dad's eyes flashed with anger at the guard but then he turned back to me.

"You have nothing to be sorry for," he said, his eyes crinkling in the corners.

His smile was genuine.

I grinned back.

"So, when I read about your bangs, I couldn't picture it," he said. "It's . . . different."

I snorted.

"You're one to talk," I said jokingly, nodding at the mop draped down his back. "Your hair is longer than mine now. Do they not have barbers in here? You're starting to look like a mountain man."

Dad chuckled as he pulled on his hair, which had grown past his shoulders.

"You have a beard now, too," I said, not adding that I hated it. Even though I did.

"All a part of my latest disguise," he said, winking at me.

"Which is?"

"Deranged crazy guy nobody wants to mess with?" he said with a shrug. "People in here tend to leave Crazy Tom alone."

"Well, you're doing a good job," I said. "And Crazy Tom works out I see?"

Despite the ill-fitting prison-issued clothing, I'd still noticed almost instantly that Dad had lost all of his softness. All of the pudge that had made him nothing much to look at had been replaced with lean muscle. His arms were the only body part I could see, but even they were toned.

"He does." Dad nodded, resisting the urge to flex his muscles. It would've been something he'd have done before. Goofing around and not caring who saw it. But not now. Not here.

"Planning on competing in some bodybuilding contests?" I asked jokingly.

"Absolutely. And I'll win every single one," Dad said, playing along. "But what I really like are the outfits I get to wear. You just wait. Soon I'll be the next Rock. I'll be famous."

"You're already famous," I teased.

"Ah, right," he said, his face dropping a little.

I immediately felt guilty for making him look like that.

"But enough about me, let's talk about you!" he said, forcing a smile.

He was off his game. Ordinarily, he would've done a better job of hiding what he was really feeling from me.

Maybe he was just sick of hiding what he was feeling from everyone.

"Thank you for sending me your journal," he said, placing his hands down on the table between us. "I loved reading about everything you've been up to. You're such a great writer, too! Who knew? And of course, I came off rather well, if I do say so myself."

I rolled my eyes at him.

"You're only saying that because I'm your daughter," I

argued. "And you have to like what I wrote—I'm *just like you*. Only cuter."

"Well, that's true," he said with a laugh. Then his eyes turned down to stare at his hands and his voice got quieter. "But I've been thinking . . . maybe you should focus more on being just like you and less like me."

I blinked at him, not quite understanding the words that were coming out of his mouth.

"Huh?" I asked, scrunching up my face in confusion.

"It's just, after reading your journal and hearing about you and your friend pulling the job on that Miles character, it got me thinking that . . . maybe it's time for you to retire."

I stared at him blankly now.

"What are you talking about?" I asked.

My dad looked up at me then and I could see that he was struggling with what to say next. But I didn't care. If it was such a struggle for him, then maybe he shouldn't be saying it.

"Look, I loved traveling around with you all those years. And you were the best partner I've ever had—and that's even with your mom thrown into the ring," he said, trying to lighten things up. "But now I'm in here, and you've got your whole life ahead of you out there. Why not put the past on a shelf and be a normal kid for once?"

"Because being normal sucks," I said angrily. "Did you not read the part of my journal where I talked about my useless classes at school and the lame girls who are awful to everyone?"

"I did," he responded, trying to keep his tone even. "And I was proud of how you handled it. I just think that maybe you could redirect all the effort you put into doing a job and stand up for people . . . at your school. Maybe put the thief side of you away for a while."

I shook my head.

"I can't believe it," I said incredulously.

"Frankie, I just want what's best for you—"

"What's best for *me* is for you to not be in *here*," I spatted. "What's best for *me* is for life to go back to normal. For me to have my old dad back, and for you to not ask me to change who I am. That's what would be best for me."

My dad's mouth was hanging open in surprise. He hadn't expected my outburst. Heck, *I* hadn't expected my outburst. But here we were.

"Frankie—"

I could feel hot tears starting to form in the corners of my eyes and didn't want to be here when they began to pour out.

"No, I get it. You don't want me to be like *you* anymore," I said, standing up clumsily. My voice was shaky and it was giving away more emotion than I cared to share with a roomful of strangers. I could see the hurt and guilt on my dad's face, but I was too upset to care.

Good.

He *should* be hurt by what he'd said. Because I was hurt too.

"You want me to be a normal kid, Dad?" I asked him, slamming my hands down on the table. "Fine. How's this for normal kid behavior."

And then I turned around and stormed out of the room, leaving him calling out after me.

Entry Nine

I was eight years old when I pulled my first heist.

It had taken me over two years of hard work, pleading and studying my dad's every move to finally convince him I was ready. And when I did, I was so excited that I didn't sleep for a week. Which, in hindsight, was not a smart move since you need to be on top of your game to break into someone's place without making any mistakes.

Now, I always go to bed early the night before a job.

"So, what are we gonna take?" I asked, practically jumping up and down when Dad had told me he'd finally chosen a target. "Jewelry? Money? A pair of limited edition Yeezys?"

"Better than all of that," Dad said, his face lit up with excitement.

What could be better than a pair of Yeezys?

"We're going to steal . . . a barrel!"

For a second I thought maybe I was hearing things.

"Wait—huh?" I asked.

"We're going to steal a *barrel*," he repeated with the same level of enthusiasm as before.

same level of enthusiasm as before.

"Um, why?" I asked, confused. "Is it full of gold or something?"

My dad smiled.

"Something," he said.

Then he proceeded to lay out the entire plan, part by part for me. Before he was even finished explaining, I was fully hooked and on board.

When we arrived at a chateau in France weeks later, my stomach felt queasy. Not because I was nervous.

But because I was excited.

"I can't believe I'm finally doing this!" I squealed as we drove up.

I caught my dad grinning out of the corner of my eye. He was trying to play it cool, but I knew this was as big a moment for him as it was for me. His baby girl was officially growing up, and even if he wasn't showing it, he was as psyched as I was.

We drove up to the old castle and I pointed to a place down the street where we could park under cover of darkness. Dad nodded and pulled our truck into the spot under the building's wall, killing the engine before turning to me.

"You ready for this?" he asked me.

"I was *born* ready," I said.

Dad chuckled, but then his face grew serious.

"I've gotta ask you one more time—and I really want you to think about your answer before you give it—are you sure you want to do this? Right now is like that poem we just read the other day. The one about the two roads and which path to take? This is like that."

"Well, which road's better?" I asked simply.

"Neither is better or worse," he said. "They're just different. And you can't know where they'll lead until you're already too far out. You just have to listen to your gut and follow your own compass."

I glanced up at the castle and stared at the outline in the night. Then I looked back at my dad.

"I want to take the road you're taking," I said, absolutely sure this was the right answer for me.

Dad resisted the urge to smile in victory and reached over to squeeze my shoulder instead.

"All right," he said, getting out of the car and attaching his utility belt around his waist. "Let's do this then."

I climbed out after him, tossing the bag full of tools over my shoulder.

It was heavy. About fifteen pounds. And given that I only weighed fifty soaking wet, it was a lot. But I was prepared for it. I'd walked around with the bag on my back everywhere I'd gone for the past week.

Now it felt more a part of me than a purse would.

"You know, that speech back there was great and all, but you kind of sealed my fate when you named me Frankie," I said, walking in the opposite direction of the castle.

"What are you talking about? Frankie's a great name!"

Dad argued, grabbing the end of a large, flexible hose from the back of the car and connecting it to a latch on his belt. He gave it a tug and it unwound with ease from the spool it was attached to and made a little pile at his feet.

"Hey, I'm on board with it," I said, throwing up my hands defensively. "I'm just saying that if you'd wanted me to choose a different lifestyle than this, maybe you shouldn't have named me after another famous thief."

"Frank Abagnale Jr. isn't just *another famous thief*," Dad corrected. "He's the *ultimate* thief. Please tell me I don't have to educate you on him again."

"No, I get it," I said, cutting him off before the lecture began. "He's the man. What I mean is that when you name your daughter after someone, what else do you expect her to be? Of course I was going to become a thief. It's my namesake."

Dad turned his back to the wall and placed his bag on the ground. Then he crouched into a squat in front of it, looking like a cheerleader on those ESPN competitions.

"Fair enough," he said, putting one hand on top of the other, palms facing up. "But you always have a choice, Frankie. Namesake or not, I'd never push you to do this. The life of a thief isn't for the faint of heart."

I took a running three steps and then put my foot into his hands, pushed off of his shoulders, and kept my body tight as he tossed me up over his head and onto the top of the wall.

"Duh," I said, swinging one leg over until I was straddling it. "But what else was I supposed to grow up to be? A doctor? A teacher? Yeah, right."

"If you get your own protégé one day, you'll pretty much become a teacher, you know," Dad pointed out. "And I bet you'll be good at it."

It was Dad's turn to take a run at the wall and I watched as he ran two steps up the side and threw his hands up to grip the top edge. Then, without missing a beat, he popped his body up so it was level with mine.

"Nice," I said, before slipping down the other side and dropping to the ground gracefully. "And she sticks the landing."

Dad jumped down next, performing a little forward roll as he landed. The hose trailed behind him as he moved.

"Show-off," I said sarcastically.

Dad pulled out a little black box the size of a walkie-talkie and pushed a button. As soon as the light went on, I knew all the cameras in the area had been scrambled, and we were free to move about undetected. The guards on watch would obviously know something was up with the monitors, but by the time they decided to come check it out, we'd already be gone.

"Did Mom think I'd be a thief?" I asked him as we made our way down the grass-covered hill to the chateau cellars.

There was a pause behind me. "She wasn't sure. When

you were little, you used to tell her you wanted to be a mouse when you grew up. Or an ear, nose, and throat doctor."

I made a face. Why the heck had I wanted to be that kind of doctor? With all the snot and ear wax and stuff? Gross.

I totally got the mouse thing, though. I still really like cheese.

"Mom didn't care *what* you wanted to be as long as you chose your own passion," Dad continued as we moved across the grounds. "She didn't get much freedom in that when she was growing up, and she didn't want the same for you. With that said, she saw a lot of herself in you. Even as a baby, you seemed to excel at certain things that made her wonder if you got more than just her looks."

We arrived at the cellar within minutes, and Dad began to work his magic on the lock.

"So, she'd be happy with my choice then?" I asked him, not wanting to sound too needy. Even at the age of eight, I guarded my emotions a bit. It was something I'd learned through watching Dad and his colleagues who were in the business. Emotions could give people something to prey on. Because when people knew you cared about something—a person, objects, approval, love— they also knew what to use against you.

Having emotions made you human. Showing your emotions could be your undoing.

With that said, Dad had always made it clear that

there wasn't anything I could do that would disappoint—or shock—him. And he never judged. Because chances are he'd been there himself.

Dad swung open the cellar door and took a little bow, to which I clapped silently. Then he gestured for me to go ahead before turning on the little headlamp he was wearing so we could see where we were going.

"Are you kidding? Your mom would be so proud of you, Frankie," he said. "But not because you decided to follow in our footsteps. She'd be proud because you're blazing your own trail."

I looked down at my feet as I descended the cellar stairs, listening to the echoes my shoes made as I went.

"I'm not really blazing anything yet," I countered as I reached the bottom and then stared into the cavernous room. "This whole plan was yours. I'm just along for the ride."

I slid the bag from my shoulders and rummaged inside until I found what I was looking for. Pulling the grappling hook launcher out, I nearly dropped it as I handed it over to him. It was actually what had made my bag so freaking heavy. But it was integral to our plan, so I hadn't complained when it had literally weighed me down.

"It's not just my *plan*," Dad argued, checking the launcher to make sure all the gear was in place. "This next part is all you."

I grinned because he was right.

Retrieving a container of flour and a handheld fan from the bag, I stood back up and looked off into the darkness. Then, I turned on the fan, took a handful of the white powder, and watched as it swirled all over the room.

The particles quickly exposed the infrared lights coming from the room's alarm system which zig-zagged along the floor, making it impossible for someone to cross without setting it off.

Around us, the whole place was made out of large chunks of rock, and it felt like we were in a dungeon instead of a room that stored casks of expensive brandy. Though the alcohol was sold by the bottle, it was made by the barrel.

And that was why we were here.

Dad had learned through the grapevine that this particular alcohol company was about to launch a cognac that would retail for $5,000 a bottle. One of the most expensive of its kind.

So, why were we after it?

Because a bottle of the stuff held 750 milliliters of liquid gold.

But a barrel held nearly 160,000 milliliters.

If you're fast at math, you know that that's worth . . . well, a heck of a lot of money.

And as I stood there in the cellar I counted at least twenty-four barrels in front of us.

"I'm thinking . . . *there*," I said, pointing to a spot on the ceiling in the middle of the room.

Dad gave a thumbs-up and took aim at the rocky place on the ceiling that split the distance between us and the first set of barrels. The brown wooden casks were stacked on top of each other, four barrels high, and stood in three separate rows down the length of the cavernous room. All I needed to do was get to the closest one.

I held up my thumb to Dad, the signal that he should let loose the grappling hook launcher, and then watched as the four-pronged metal blades soared through the air before embedding into the rock above us.

"How did you know you wanted to be a thief?" I asked as he tested out the rope to make sure it was really stuck in there, and then handed it to me. As much as we talked about our line of work, I'd never really asked him this basic question before.

Dad took the hose from his belt and attached it to mine. Then I climbed back up a few steps and gripped the rope in my hands.

"How did I know I wanted to be a thief . . . ," Dad mused out loud. "Well, your grandmother Rose used to say I was mischievous from the start. I was always obsessed with breaking in to—and out of—things. There wasn't a kid gate or lock I couldn't get around. And then when your uncle Scotty arrived, it became even more apparent that I was the robber to his cop."

I laughed because Uncle Scotty *had* turned out to be a cop in the end. And for as much as Dad stole over his lifetime, his brother was working on stopping other bad guys from stealing stuff, too. I guess in a weird way, they sort of canceled each other out.

"I suppose in the end, I just always knew who I was supposed to be," he finished.

"I get that," I said, nodding. And it was true. There was something about all this that just felt . . . right. I couldn't explain it other than it seemed natural that I was here.

Like this was what I was born to do.

I gathered the excess rope so it wouldn't drag across the floor, and Dad held up the hose behind me, ready to feed it. Then with a deep breath, I leaned back and jumped into the darkness.

Soaring across the room in that moment was what I imagined it was like for normal kids when they climbed on a rope swing at a lake or river. Only, there was no bailing out, dropping into the water. Because my landing had to be precisely timed and executed so that I'd end up on top of the closest barrel and not on the floor below.

The experience was exhilarating, scary, fun, and incredibly freeing.

And lasted all of three seconds.

As my feet touched the wood barrel on the other side, I swayed a bit until I was sure I had my balance, and then turned around to face my dad. Feeling a bit smug over my execution, I threw my arms up in triumph.

And then I may or may not have done a little victory dance.

"Careful, Frankie," Dad warned, though he seemed to be getting a kick out of watching me.

I waved my hand at him dismissively.

"I could do this with my eyes closed," I said, clenching them shut as I said it.

"Please don't," Dad said with a groan.

"Sorry, Dad. Can't rein me in," I said, continuing to wiggle around.

Just as I was copying a dance move I'd seen on YouTube, I somehow stepped down wrong and instantly began to fall. Circling my arms through the air wildly, I tried to steady myself, but it was too late. So I did the only thing I could think of and collapsed onto the barrel to keep from ending up on the floor.

I continued to grip the barrel, hands trembling and face smashed against the grainy wood, until I was positive I hadn't set off any alarms. Finally, I lifted my eyes sheepishly.

"Okay, maybe you can rein me in a little," I mumbled.

Dad didn't have to tell me it had been a rookie mistake. I already knew it.

Standing up again—this time on shakier legs and with a healthy amount of fear and embarrassment—I focused on the final phase of our plan.

Getting what we came here for.

I held up the drill I'd brought, and gave the trigger a pull before leaning over the side of the barrel and finding a spot I liked at the bottom. Then, slowly I drilled into the cask.

It cut through the wood easier than I'd expected it to

70

and barely took any pressure on my part to get through. When I felt the familiar give, I stopped the drill, detached the hose from my belt, and positioned the end next to where the drill was plugging the hole I'd made.

With both hands at the ready, I quickly withdrew the drill while simultaneously plugging the hole with the hose.

There was no way to keep at least some of the amber liquid from spilling out. Luckily, it wasn't too bad, just a few splashes onto the barrel below and some on my hands. I wiped them off on my pants and then made sure the hose was fully attached.

"Ready," I announced when I was satisfied that it was all in place.

"Okay," Dad called back. "Let's turn her on then."

I pressed the tiny silver button near the opening of the hose and watched as the formerly limp line began to fill up.

"It's working," I said quietly, before letting out a little laugh. Even though it was going as planned, it still left me in awe. "It's working!"

I knew through all the dry runs we'd done before tonight that when I'd pressed the button on the hose, it had triggered the pump back at the truck to syphon all the brandy out of the barrel.

Within minutes it had drained nearly 160,000 milliliters of cognac.

And just like that, we'd become millionaires.

Find the mark. Devise the plan. Execute the plan. Disappear rich.

It was a ridiculously simple business model that was difficult to pull off, yet somehow we'd just done it.

"Congratulations, Frankie," Dad said as I rejoined him on the other side of the room. "You just pulled off your first job. How does it feel?"

"Great!" I said. My whole body hummed with excitement.

The truth was, I felt invincible. I felt alive. I felt more like me than I ever had before.

And that's when it became clear: This was who I was.

I was a thief.

Entry Ten

So, you can see why I was so freaking annoyed when Dad suggested I be something else.

Someone else.

Not once had I *ever* asked him to change who he was. Even when he went and got caught by the FBI and ended up in prison and I had to go live with a cop.

Even then, I'd never suggested he give up the one thing that made him, *him*.

And so, when he told me maybe I should just be a normal kid? It was like a kick in the stomach.

That man in the prison visitor's room, sitting there across from me . . . that wasn't *my dad*. My dad, the infamous Tom Lorde, would never have asked me to leave our life behind. He'd never suggest I change. Heck, he would've helped me plan my next job.

That guy in there had been an impostor. A doppelganger they'd replaced him with maybe. Either way, he was not the guy I grew up with.

The one who'd taught me I was perfect just the way I was.

And I certainly wasn't going to change who I was for someone I didn't even recognize anymore.

That's why I'd gotten so upset.

That's why I'd stormed out.

And that's why, in that moment, I decided I was definitely pulling my next job. . . .

Like, now.

Nobody was reining me in anymore.

Entry Eleven

Reading back over my last entry, I'll admit it was a bit melo-dramatic. . . .

But only a little bit.

For the most part, I stand behind everything I said.

And I'm still going to take down that exotic trade jerk. Whoever it is.

If anyone deserves it, they do.

But I'll also rein in the drama.

Mostly because it has dawned on me that it's the behavior of a typical kid my age.

And I refuse to turn into that.

Entry Twelve

Ollie stood there in my kitchen staring at me with his mouth wide open.

He didn't move.

Just gaped as if in shock.

And he might've been. Even I'd been a bit stunned when I'd looked in the mirror after the transformation.

"I think you finally did it, Frankie," Uncle Scotty said, watching everything unfold as he drank his morning coffee while leaning against the counter. "You've rendered Oliver speechless. I didn't think it was possible, but, well . . . congrats."

"What?" I asked nonchalantly to Ollie as I poured cereal into my bowl.

He finally slammed his mouth shut and swallowed the drool that had been pooling at the corners. Then he shook his head in disbelief.

"What do you mean, *what*?" he asked me, his brain officially kicking into high gear. "What did you *do*, Frankie?!"

I scowled at him. "Gee, thanks."

So, I'd done a little something different with my hair.

Okay, *a lot* of something different to my hair.

So, sue me.

I held up my spoon and peered at my reflection. I had to admit, it was . . . bold.

When I'd walked into the salon, I'd found the most edgy girl there and plopped down in her seat without asking if she was free.

"I want something totally different," I'd said, staring at my boring hairstyle in the mirror.

"Cool," was all the girl said back.

Then she started cutting. When she discovered I was a natural blond—and not just blond, but icy blond—she just about died.

And then she dyed my hair . . .

. . . back to its original color.

I'd walked out of the place a few hours later with a punky new 'do and an attitude to match.

Ollie placed his hand on the back of a chair as if he needed the support.

"I just have so many questions," he said slowly. "One, *why*? Two, *why didn't you let me do it*? You know I live for a good makeover. Three, did you break up with someone and not tell me about it? Four, was this a crazy Britney Spears sort of situation? Okay, your turn."

I raised my eyebrow at him as I continued to crunch on my breakfast instead of answering his questions.

"Good luck with that one," Uncle Scotty muttered as he put his mug into the sink. "I've been trying to get her to talk since Friday, but she's like Fort Knox."

Ollie's eyes widened as he put two and two together.

My uncle started off across the room and leaned toward Ollie as he passed. "Let me know if you find anything out," he muttered

"Will do," Ollie responded absently, his mind already elsewhere.

Once I heard the familiar click of the front door and Uncle Scotty starting up his car, I finally dared to look over at my friend.

"Well?" he asked. "What drama are we looking at, here?"

"No drama," I answered easily.

"No drama? Yeah right," he answered. "Extreme makeovers of this level happen for a reason. What's yours?

"I just wanted to get back to my roots," I said with a shrug.

"Literally?" Ollie said, sitting down across from me.

"Yeah," I said, sticking my chin out. "You don't like it?"

He reached out and touched my hair. Well, what was left of it. My former bob haircut and bangs had been replaced with a buzz cut around most of my head with the exception of a longer, faux-hawk style in the front.

It might've been a bit flashy, but I sort of loved it. And it was the most I'd felt like myself since I'd arrived in this town.

No one was going to try to control this version of me, that was for sure.

"It's a little pixie," Ollie mused, walking around me

as he examined my new look. "It's a little punk. It's hard to pin down. Which I'd say describes you to a *T*."

"Why, thank you," I said, pleased that somebody seemed to understand me.

"With that said . . . ," he continued.

Uh-oh.

"There's gotta be a story behind it. I need to hear that story," he concluded.

I paused, the spoon halfway to my mouth.

"No, you don't," I said.

"Yes," he argued. "I do."

"Nah."

"But I *insist*," he said, giving me what I think was supposed to be his *I'm serious* look. It really just made him appear constipated.

I placed both my hands on the tabletop and pushed myself up.

"Fine!" I grumbled and let out a big breath. "But only because you'll just annoy me until I do anyway. And I need something from you, too."

"Goody!" Ollie said, clapping his hands together giddily because he was getting his way.

The truth was, I was always going to tell him. It was just a matter of when.

"Come on," I said, motioning for him to follow me.

On the way upstairs, I gave Ollie the Cliffs Notes version of my visit with Dad. When I was finished, I plopped down on my bed and buried my head, not wanting to see his face when he took his beloved Tom Lorde's side of the argument.

After a few seconds of silence, he just said, "That's crappy. What was your dad thinking?"

My head shot up from its place in my comforter.

"Wait—you agree with *me*?"

As soon as it was out of my mouth, I regretted it. The words sounded so . . . *needy*. And I *hated* needy. But until now, I hadn't realized how much I'd been hoping for his support.

Ollie looked at me like I was crazy.

"*Of course*," he said. "How could *your* dad—the guy who taught you everything you know—ask you to be someone else? It's beyond hypocritical."

My heart, which had been frozen like an icicle since seeing Dad, thawed a little then.

Ollie must've seen the change in my demeanor, because he took a step toward me.

"You do realize that I'll always have your back, right?" he asked, making it clear he meant what he was saying. "I may be obsessed with Tom Lorde, but *you're* my ride or die. The one I'd follow into fire."

I turned away from him so he couldn't see the emotions building in my face.

"There's no need to be so dramatic," I said, trying to force the tightness in my throat to disappear. Then I looked down at my hands. "But I appreciate you saying it."

We were getting dangerously close to having a moment

there, and luckily Ollie sensed my reluctance. He cleared his throat and began to walk around the room, touching things as he went.

"You said you had a favor to ask before?" he said, changing the subject.

"Right," I answered, taking a few cleansing breaths before turning around to face him again. "So, the one good thing that came out of my visit with Dad is that I'm definitely going after that tiger guy. I mean, *we* are, if you're up for it."

Ollie's face lit up like Christmas morning.

"Oh, I'm up for it," he said, hardly able to hold in his excitement. "When do we start?"

"Now," I answered.

Entry Thirteen

I pushed open the double doors to the Greenwich Police Department but hesitated before crossing the threshold.

Once I did so, I knew that there was no going back.

For me or for Ollie.

"Everything okay?" Ollie asked in my ear.

I turned my head slightly to see that he was standing right behind me.

"No problem," I said, trying to act cool.

You're not turning yourself in, so stop acting so guilty, I berated myself.

"Okay, so, you know what your job is, right?" I asked him under my breath for about the fifth time since we'd left my house.

"Yes," Ollie said, sounding bored by the question. "Do you?"

I snorted at him before walking up to the front desk and waiting for someone to notice us.

"Next." A good-looking man with skin the color of cocoa motioned for us to step forward. "And how can I help you two?"

"We're here to see Detective Lorde," I said.

He turned back to the computer and typed on the keys.

"And what is this in reference to?" he asked.

"Um, it's in reference to me being his niece?" I said, not sure what else he was looking for.

His eyes left the computer and really looked at me now. He took in the shockingly white hair and raised an eyebrow.

"I know," I said, almost apologetically. "We're practically twins, right?"

He didn't laugh, but he did pick up the phone and punch in a few numbers.

"What's your name?" he asked as he waited for the call to connect.

"Frankie," I said. "He'll know who I am."

When the man still didn't laugh at my obvious wit, I turned to Ollie and rolled my eyes.

"Hey," the officer said into the phone, finally, still eyeing us suspiciously. "Yeah, so I've got a kid named Frankie here for you. She says she's your niece?"

There was a brief pause.

"Uh-huh," he said before hanging up the phone.

"Wait over there and Detective Lorde will be out in a minute," the officer said, pointing over to an empty bench near the door. Then he turned his attention away from us. "Next!"

We'd barely sat down when Uncle Scotty appeared through a side door, a worried look on his face.

"What's wrong?" he asked coming up to us.

I blinked.

"Nothing," I said, standing up. "Ollie just kept asking to see the inside of a real, live police station. We had nothing else to do. So here we are."

"Oh," Uncle Scotty said and let out the breath he'd been holding. "Okay. Don't freak me out like that."

"What? You only want me to visit when there's a crisis?" I asked him with a smirk.

"Isn't that what you're doing?" he asked, raising an eyebrow as he eyed my hair.

"It's just a haircut, people!" I exclaimed. Everyone in the waiting area turned their attention to us. "Geez, don't get it twisted."

Uncle Scotty noticed the staring, and waved for Ollie and I to follow him through the door he'd just appeared from.

"You guys can come in, but you have to be invisible, okay?" he said.

"Kinda hard to do when you're her or me," Ollie said pointing to both of us.

"Try," Uncle Scotty just said.

We might've raised a few eyebrows outside, but nobody inside the station even looked twice as we were led through the bullpen—the big, open room full of desks and officers. The officers there had seen it all.

Uncle Scotty eventually stopped at a desk and sat down, gesturing for us to do the same at the one across from his. I surveyed Uncle Scotty's workspace. It was tidy—all the odds and ends had a designated space and his papers were lined up perfectly in his inbox. There were a few action figures in the corner: Wolverine, Cyclops, Rogue, Mystique, and Gambit. Either he was an X-Men fan, or he simply liked to play with toys. My bet was on the former.

My gaze fell on a frame he had on his desktop. It was plain black wood that appeared distressed, though I doubted it was homemade. And it was dusty. It had been there awhile. I was surprised to see the picture that was in it, and leaned forward to take a closer look.

It was of me and Uncle Scotty, sitting together in the back of his truck. I was younger than I am now. By several years. My hair was long. All the way down my back, and the same bright white it was currently. I didn't have bangs. I was wearing a crooked smile on my face and was leaning against my uncle sheepishly.

I could remember the day clearly.

It was the last time we'd visited Uncle Scotty. Before the whole FBI hunt and everything.

Dad had taken the photo.

It had been a great day.

Uncle Scotty saw me staring at it and cleared his throat.

"We should take another one," he suggested. "Now that you've got your new haircut and all."

I let out a little smile at the gentle teasing. With adults, you had to dole out the victories sporadically so they didn't get big heads about things. But Uncle Scotty had been oddly cool about not prying about my visit with Dad. He hadn't even freaked out when I'd chopped all my hair off.

At least, he hadn't freaked out on me.

"Speaking of," Ollie chimed in, and caught my uncle's eye as subtly as he could muster. This was the hardest part for Ollie, because subtlety was not his strong suit. He leaned over toward Uncle Scotty conspiratorially. "I might have the info you've been looking for."

Then he darted his eyes toward me wildly.

Oh, Ollie.

"Okay," Uncle Scotty said, not totally sure what was going on.

"Detective?" Ollie then asked loudly. I was pretty sure the whole room could hear him. "Take me to my holding cell."

"Just call me Scotty, Oliver," he reminded him with a sigh.

"Only if you call me Ollie," my friend responded seriously. "My mom's the only one who calls me Oliver and that's mostly when I'm in trouble. *Now about those jail cells . . .*"

"Uh, sure," Uncle Scotty said. Then he looked over at me. "You wanna see the cells, too, Frankie?"

"Huh?" I said, acting like I was only just tuning in.

"Your uncle's gonna lock me up," Ollie said enthusiastically. "Wanna come?"

"Not even a little bit," I said dismissively.

"Hey, Uncle Scotty, can I check my email on this computer?" I asked as he started to stand up from his chair. He paused and looked at me curiously. I held up my phone in response. "I don't have any service in here."

Uncle Scotty nodded at the computer behind me.

"That's the intern desk," he said. "You can use that."

"Thanks," I said in response, turning my back to them and starting to type on the keyboard. "You two have fun!"

"Oh, we will," Ollie said, jumping up giddily.

I waited until I heard them walk away to close out of Google and get to work.

The Greenwich Police Department logo flashed up on the screen as soon as I moved the mouse. Right underneath it were two boxes.

USERNAME:

PASSWORD:

This probably would've stopped the average person from going any further, but thankfully I knew a thing or two about breaking into places I wasn't authorized to be.

And an internal police department database was no different.

Most people kept their usernames and passwords in readily accessible places. For computers, this meant a note of some sort kept near the screen or something scribbled down on a stray paper that was kept in a nearby drawer. Occasionally it would be hidden on the underside of the desk, so that it's out of sight, but still easily available.

The sign-in info was almost embarrassingly easy to find. And if I was positive I wouldn't need to break into their system again in the future, I would've given Uncle Scotty a heads-up that they needed to be more careful.

My eyes landed on the bright yellow sticky note tacked up on a cork board just to the right of the computer.

USERNAME: Intern7

PASSWORD: 5tb18h!g79

Thank you, Intern7.

I logged in and started my search.

I'd told Ollie to stall as long as he could, but I knew I only had a short amount of time before they came back.

I typed in Christian Miles's name and clicked on his file. Everything about his arrest was in there. The hidden treasure room. The security tapes of his confessions. The transcriptions of his interviews with the feds. The list of items confiscated from his house.

I scanned the list and found what I'd been looking for.

1 white Bengal tiger, approximately four and a half years of age, 515 pounds. Name is Opulence. In good health, well taken care of. Found living on property. Being sent to animal rescue nearby. More Art37.

I clicked on the link at the end, hoping it would lead to something more.

It did.

I looked up from the screen even though it was turned away from the room and only I could see what was on it.

I clicked on the transcription marked as Article 37.

And then began to smile triumphantly.

Agent Tripe: A white Bengal tiger was found on your property. Were you aware of the existence of this animal?

Christian Miles: I was.

Agent Tripe: And were you aware that it is illegal to own a dangerous cat in Greenwich?

Christian Miles: Opulence isn't dangerous.

Agent Tripe: Are you aware that it is illegal to own a tiger in Greenwich without a special license?

Christian Miles: Oh, really?

Agent Tripe: Yes.

Christian Miles: Interesting.

Agent Tripe: You might have gleaned this by the level of difficulty it would have taken to obtain him.

Christian Miles: Her. Opulence is a female. And I don't often trouble myself with trivial information such as where I get my pets.

Agent Tripe: So, you are unaware of who supplied you with the animal?

Christian Miles: Why does it matter?

Agent Tripe: Because catching a criminal embedded in the illegal animal trade business might be of some interest to us.

Christian Miles: *How* interesting?

Agent Tripe: If you were to give up your dealer, we might be able to work something out. A few luxuries in your cell maybe?

Christian Miles: I'd need it in writing.

Agent Tripe: Of course.

Paperwork is presented with offer to Christian Miles in exchange for information.

Agent Tripe: Who provided you with the tiger?

Christian Miles: I believe his name is Sam Brasko.

Agent Tripe: The socialite?

Christian Miles: I don't pay attention to what people do in their spare time.

Agent Tripe: Did Sam Brasko say where he procured the tiger?

Christian Miles: No.

Agent Tripe: Are you sure?

Christian Miles: Quite. Why should I care where he got her? I pay other people to worry about that stuff. Listen, I'm not going to do all your work for you. If you want to know about the man, do your own homework.

Agent Tripe: Interview suspended at 3:17 p.m.

"Frankie, you have to see this picture!" Ollie practically squealed as he and my uncle walked across the room. "I was like Al Capone all locked up. My mom's gonna freak when she sees it!"

I glanced briefly at the screen in front of me and then up at them. They'd be by my side in five.

Four.

Three.

Two.

"Still checking email?" Uncle Scotty asked as he turned the corner to peek at my computer screen.

Panic filled Ollie's eyes.

"Wait!" he exclaimed quickly, trying to distract Uncle Scotty from seeing what I was doing. "Handcuff me! You didn't handcuff me before. I have to have a picture of that! Let's go back—"

But Uncle Scotty was already surveying what I'd been doing and he immediately began to frown.

"Solitaire?" he asked.

I shrugged. "I'm winning."

"How did that get on there?" he muttered.

"It's a computer, I think it comes with it?" I offered. "Either that or it's been a slow year for whoever sits here."

"That's weird, we haven't had an intern for months," Uncle Scotty said passively. "I mostly use it as a place to seat people when I bring them in."

I clicked the game closed and the GPD landing page popped up again. Then I stood up from the chair and shoved my hands into my coat pockets.

"Well, we'll let you get back to kicking butt and taking names," I said.

"What are you two up to the rest of the afternoon?" Uncle Scotty asked curiously as we began to walk away.

"Heading to the library," I answered.

"Work or fun?" he asked, though I could tell his mind was already back on work.

I fingered the piece of paper that I'd slipped into my pocket with a single name on it: Sam Brasko.

"A little bit of both," I said over my shoulder as we headed out the door.

Entry Fourteen

So, the Lorde had a new target.

I also had a renewed energy I hadn't felt since the last time we were hatching a plan. I felt free. Alive. Like I wasn't itching to get out of my skin for once.

I felt like me.

Even heading into research mode was exciting.

Not for Ollie so much. He hated the library with what seemed like an unreasonable amount of passion. Something about a history of paper cuts and the smell of books? I think it was actually that he hated anywhere that required him to be quiet. And possibly the librarian, Ms. Harriet Smars. She was so old and frail, he was convinced she was superhuman. And not in a good way.

"Her eyes follow you everywhere you go," he whispered to me as we walked past her post at the main desk. "And I'm pretty sure she can read minds."

I looked over at her and nodded hello.

She gave me a curt smile but narrowed her eyes at Ollie.

"See?" he hissed, trying to hide his round body behind mine. It didn't work. "I was just wondering if she sucks the life force out of kids who turn in their books late and that's what's *really* keeping her alive since she's clearly two hundred years old by now . . . and now she's glaring at me!"

"Well, maybe you should start thinking nice thoughts," I suggested, finding his bizarre fear of a little old lady funny.

He squinted his eyes while staring at her.

She scowled and then huffed before turning back to checking books back in.

Ollie turned his wide eyes toward me.

"That's it," he said. "I'm doomed."

"You should probably start planning what you want on your tombstone now," I agreed, nodding. "In the meantime, let's focus on things that are *really happening*. Like our new plan."

Ollie rubbed his hands together like he was a villain.

"It's not an *evil* plan," I said as I sat down at the farthest computer cube in the building. This spot was perfect for recon work since nobody could see what we were looking up and our searches couldn't be traced back to us.

As much as Ollie hated the Greenwich Library, it was one of the best resources in our line of work.

"So, what's the plan? What disguises do I need? Please tell me I get a starring role this time," Ollie said, sitting down on the tabletop next to the computer screen.

"Looks like we're going after . . ." I took out the piece of paper and read from it. "Sam Brasko."

"Hold up," Ollie said, sounding shocked. "*The* Sam

Brasko? Socialite and overall party boy, Sam Brasko? As in the grandson of the man who runs the Huntington Diamond Empire? The one worth, like, a bazillion dollars?"

"So, you've heard of him?" I said sarcastically.

"Heard of him?" Ollie scoffed. "I *majored* in him and his sister. Frankie, we don't need Google for this. Let's go get a frappaccino and I'll fill you in on everything you want to know about them."

"Them?" I asked, confused.

Ollie jumped down from the desk and pulled me into a standing position.

"Oh, Frankie," he said, with a flick of his wrist. "This is where I shine."

• • •

"Okay, you have your ice-blended whatever," I said, handing him the drink that was more a dessert than anything.

"Mmmm," Ollie said, taking a big pull off the straw. Then he looked down at the cup. "No whipped cream?"

"Start talking," I commanded, picking up my own drink and taking a sip.

My brain seemed to say, *Ahhhhh*, as the caffeine hit my system. Usually I went for decaf, but today I opted for the real thing.

"As you wish," Ollie said licking some chocolate off his finger before putting his drink down. "Here's the E! *True Hollywood Story* of Sam and Emma Brasko."

"I don't need—" I started to say, but Ollie had already begun to talk.

"Sam and Emma Brasko were worth billions the day they were born," Ollie started. "The first and only grandchildren of billionaire diamond manufacturer James Huntington II, Sam and Emma were literally born into royalty."

"*They're* the heirs to Huntington Diamonds?" I asked, surprised. "Why didn't I know that?"

"Probably because they've never used the Huntington name," Ollie explained. "The old man had a falling-out with his daughter while she was pregnant with the twins. When Sam and Emma were born, their mother forbid Huntington to meet them until they were about eight, when she and her father supposedly reconciled."

"Hmmm, I've never robbed twins before," I said, even more interested than I'd been before. "Are they close?"

"Attached at the hip," he answered. "Literally. Apparently, Emma and Sam were surgically detached at birth, though I have a feeling that's just an urban legend. Either way, they stood by each other's sides through good times and bad. And they've had their share of bad times."

"Like?" I prompted, knowing he was enjoying the theatrics of all of this.

"Well, let's just say that they started hitting the club scene young," Ollie said. "And the paparazzi followed them everywhere they went. Which meant scandal galore—you name it, they did it."

"How do you know all this?"

"How do you *not*?" Ollie clapped back.

"Um, because people aren't as interested in the stupid things Americans do as you think they are," I answered. "When we were abroad, we never heard about the news back here, except for the really big stuff. Like, Obama becoming president."

"Sam and Emma *were* big news! Whatever, can I get back to my story?" Ollie said, annoyed I'd interrupted him.

I gestured for him to continue and fought the urge to laugh at how serious he was taking this.

"Anyway," he continued, glaring at me before going on. "After a bunch of years on the scene, the spotlight got a little too hot for them and they both flamed out, damaging the family name. Word has it, that's when Grandpa Huntington put his foot down and told them they either had to move away and get their lives together or he'd write them out of his will. So, they bought one of the biggest mansions here in Greenwich and moved in together to lay low."

"They live *together*? As adults?" I asked, raising an eyebrow. "That's a little weird."

"They're twins," Ollie said, shrugging like it was a valid answer. "Besides, their house is ridiculous. They both have their own separate wings. I bet they rarely even run into each other."

"You know where they live?" I asked.

"Everyone here knows where they live," Ollie said. "It's hard to keep a place like that hidden. Though the twins have done a pretty good job at being low-key. People rarely see them around town. But I guess you can make that happen when you have a full-time staff to do everything for you."

"And the party twins are supposed to be the masterminds behind an animal trade ring?" I asked, skeptically.

"So, you think it isn't true?" Ollie asked.

"True or not, Miles gave Sam's name to the feds for a reason," I concluded. "We just need to figure out why."

"And we're gonna do that how?" Ollie asked.

I drank what was left of my coffee and then got up.

"Sorry, Ollie," I said, smiling deviously. "It's back to the library."

Entry Fifteen

BILLIONAIRE BRASKOS A RARE BREED.

The headline was the first to come up when I googled the twins' names with the word *animals*. According to more than a few news outlets, the twins weren't just your average, everyday animal lovers.

They were fur-natics.

And they had the press to prove it. There were a batch of photos of the two alongside their beloved dogs, Titan and Lady Godiva, at a fundraising event for Best Friends Animal Society in New York City. And then an interview for Paws & Claws TV where they told funny and heartwarming stories of their furry friends. Emma's Pomeranian had his own Instagram account with over 2.3 million followers. Sam was on the cover of *Hamptons* magazine, standing alongside his Great Dane, who was practically the size of a miniature horse.

"What is all of this?" I asked out loud as I looked at yet another interview with the former socialites fawning all over their pets.

"Ooh, click on that one!" Ollie exclaimed and leaned over my shoulder to do it before I could protest. "This one just came out last week."

The video Ollie had chosen was a clip from one of those entertainment news shows where they covered red carpet events for movie premiers. This one was for the latest film about a dog. Or dogs. It wasn't totally clear. What was clear was Sam and Emma's support of it.

"I hear we have some pretty big animal lovers in the house tonight!" a perky reporter said into her microphone. "And here are two of them right now!"

A thirty-something guy sauntered into the frame, followed by a woman the same age. She was dressed in a yellow ruffled dress that extended nearly to her ankles, which were tied up with trendy gladiator sandals. Her hair was long and loose, soft golden curls framing her sun-kissed face. If she was wearing makeup, it wasn't much. Not that she needed it. Then she briefly waved to the crowd before turning her attention back to the man, placing her arm on his shoulder, and leaning in to say something to him that the microphone didn't pick up.

The guy laughed, his head tipping back effortlessly as his beachy hair gently brushed the top of his shoulders. He looked like he could've been an actor in the movie they were about to see, dressed in his fitted jeans and an ivory-colored sweater. Definitely didn't look like your typical trust fund kid.

But money and time could hide a lot of demons.

"Sam and Emma Brasko, so good to have you out tonight!" the reporter said as the brother-sister team finally turned their attention to her.

"Excited to be here," Emma said, in a laid-back kind of drawl.

"Hey," Sam said, his charm oozing out of every pore. Then he smiled at the female reporter and she giggled.

Actually giggled. On air.

She pulled herself together quickly, though, clearing her throat and saying, "So, who do we have here?"

The reporter leaned over to scratch the head of Emma's pooch, who was dressed to the nines in a cute little tutu and matching bow. But as her fingers got close, the dog began to growl.

"This is Lady Godiva," Emma offered, showing her fluffy pooch off. She either didn't notice or flat-out ignored the fact that the reporter had recoiled at the dog's less-than-friendly hello.

"She's . . . darling," the reporter said, forcing a smile.

"And where's the famed Titan today?" She turned back to Sam, a real grin crossing her face.

"Aw, he's back at home," Sam said, running his hand through his hair. "He'd block the view of the audience if I'd brought him."

Everyone laughed at this, because it was true.

The dog was enormous.

"Well, maybe next time then," the reporter concluded, still laughing. Then she leaned in conspiratorially. "A little doggy told me we might be seeing a lot more of Lady Godiva and Titan in the future. Can you tell us what you have coming up?"

"Sure," Emma said, her voice slow and serene like molasses. "So, our dogs are our *lives*. We'd literally do anything for them. And we were watching a documentary on tiny houses, and noticed they would be perfect houses for our dogs. And that got us thinking, we should make a tiny dog palace for Lady Godiva and Titan, and document it for everyone to see!"

"So, is it going to be, like, a reality show with you two . . . and your dogs?" the reporter asked.

I wondered if she thought the idea was as stupid as I did.

"Lady Godiva already has a huge following on social," Emma continued. "And people are always asking what Sam and I are up to now, so we figured, two birds, right? Not that we condone throwing rocks at birds. It's just a saying."

Sam slung his arm over his sister's shoulder. Whether it was to shut her up or just a show of how close they were, you couldn't tell. Either way, Emma seemed to take the cue and leaned in to him silently.

"It's gonna be real cool," he said, sounding psyched. "Emma and I will come up with the plans for what the house will look like, and then oversee the whole operation. We might even get our hands a little dirty, too."

He winked at the reporter as he said it, who just about melted while the camera was still rolling.

"So, it'll be this cool blend of our everyday lives, and our dogs, and this house we're building them," he finished with a shrug. "There's nothing like this out there right now, so it'll be pretty groundbreaking."

Groundbreaking? Are you kidding me? The guy had just described, like, every show ever on HGTV.

I looked over at Ollie to roll my eyes, but saw that he was practically drooling over what we were watching.

And I realized with horror that Ollie was their target demographic.

"So cool," he breathed as he watched the end of the interview.

I *had* to stop all of this before Ollie was turned into a pod person.

"And that's our way in," I said, ignoring his excitement over the reality show announcement.

Ollie turned to me, confused. "You still think they're the brokers? But they're all about the animals. Why would they traffic animals if they *love* animals?"

"I guess we're going to find out," I said.

Entry Sixteen

I'd been to mansions and manors. Even to a palace or two.

But the Brasko estate was beyond.

Like, it was literally bonkers.

Before I'd seen it in person, I'd wondered how the twins could possibly hide a small zoo on their property. Now I knew. The place was enormous. The property extended almost five acres—that's roughly four football fields of space—with the living quarters only taking up a fourth of it.

So yeah, it would've been super easy for Sam and Emma to hide a zoo on a property this big.

Now we just had to find it.

"*Bonjour*, good afternoon," I said, my voice taking on an elegant French accent. "My name is Brigeet Chopin. I am from *French Fur* magazine, and we are here to do an in-depth piece on *Monsieur et Mademoiselle* Brasko? This is my assistant André. Would you please announce our arrival?"

The beefy security guard at the main gate raised an eyebrow but walked over to his desk, pushed a button and then put the phone up to his ear.

As he talked, he looked over at me again.

Shoving a hand into the pocket of my black skinny jeans, I made sure to give off the vibe that I didn't actually care what he thought of me. I picked at a piece of black lint on the fabric of my loosely tucked-in white T-shirt, and then pushed up the arm of my black leather jacket to check the time on my watch. My oversized sunglasses allowed me to see others, but they couldn't see me.

It was the disguise of a French magazine editor.

It was *my* disguise.

Days before, Ollie and I had discussed several options for getting inside the Brasko's world. We'd considered posing as an animal organization, but quickly realized there was no way we'd get the twins to admit to harming animals that way. Then Ollie had suggested we dress up as delivery people, bringing overelaborate doggy goody bags, in order to literally get our feet inside the door. But I doubted Sam and Emma were hobnobbing around with their UPS guy.

After hours of brainstorming, we'd finally agreed that the best way to really infiltrate their life was as people who were there to follow their every move.

Like, as magazine staffers doing an in-depth feature on them and their upcoming reality show. We'd walk in like the whole thing had already been set up—we'd seen on their social media that they were always complaining about their publicist, so we figured it wouldn't be a stretch that something like a feature was lost in the shuffle—and convince them we needed an all-access pass to their lives.

You know, to most accurately paint the siblings and their comeback.

Considering the film crew would be on the premises, too, we figured it would be easy to fade into the background when we needed to, and search the grounds at our leisure.

The guard took his time speaking quietly into his phone while Ollie stood beside me nervously.

"*Excusez-moi,*" I said to the man in front of us, trying to sound impatient. "Is there somebody I can speak with? A publicist maybe? We have a lot to cover and go to press in a month's time."

Then I turned to Ollie and spoke in perfect French.

The guard's face scrunched up as he realized I was no longer speaking English. Ollie was clueless too, but the guard didn't know that. If either of them *had* spoken French, they would have known that I'd said: *This man doesn't have any idea what I'm saying. I could say random words and he'll think this is a serious conversation. Octopus. Banana split. Bumfuzzle. Pie hole. Man, I should've eaten breakfast. . . .*

My faux tirade in French seemed to help give the guard the push he needed.

"Go on in," he said, motioning for us to enter the gate that had already begun to swing open. "Mr. Brasko will meet you at the residence."

"*Merci,*" I said to him, and climbed onto the back of the golf cart they used to tote visitors around the property. Between the Miles and Brasko estates, I was beginning to think it was the only way the rich traveled on their grounds.

As we drove to the house, I used the time to gather together my fake credentials: mock-ups of *French Fur* covers using photos of the duo I'd found online, an example of the type of spread we wanted to do, business cards for the magazine. It had all come together pretty quickly. So had crafting my persona. I had based Brigeet after a woman my dad and I had met during one of our travels. She was refined, trendy, and didn't much care what others thought of her. She also had zero patience for people who wasted her time.

It was so utterly French, and I loved it.

Ollie wasn't exactly the typical Frenchman, but that didn't matter. As my assistant, André, was there to assist. That meant less opportunity for him to speak in a bad French accent, which was probably better off for everyone.

"Whoa," Ollie breathed as the Brasko mansion came into view.

While you couldn't see it from the ground, the house was shaped like an oversized *M*—according to certain entertainment outlets, the *M* stood for money—and showcased columns, gargoyles, and statues all along the outside.

Inside there were reported to be 123 rooms, twenty-six bedrooms, thirty-four baths, a spa, a full-size gym that rivaled Bally, a game room, theater room, meditation sanctuary, and a night club in the basement. Along the grounds, there was a tennis court, basketball court, two Olympic-size pools, an in-ground trampoline, and a man-made lake with actual sharks.

And then, of course, the zoo . . . if there actually was one.

Before the cart had even stopped, the front door opened up and Sam Brasko walked out, barefoot in a pair of jeans, and wearing what I assumed to be a white cashmere sweater. He was holding an oversized mug of something steaming, and took a leisurely sip as he eyeballed us from the steps.

"Hello!" he called out jovially, putting his hand in the air in greeting.

I hopped off the back of the cart, making sure to take my pile of documents as I went. Ollie attempted to do the same but got caught on something on the way off.

"Ooof," he muttered, and started to wiggle around. After a few seconds of pulling and grunting, he managed to work himself free and rushed over to catch up with me.

I stopped about three feet way from Sam and gave him a subtle head nod.

"*Bonjour, Monsieur Brasko,*" I said, and leaned forward to kiss both of his cheeks.

Sam's face lit up in surprise for just a second and then leaned in to return the greeting.

"*Bonjour, mademoiselle,*" Sam replied back, his own French accent coming out.

I blinked, slightly taken aback.

"Oh! *Tu parles français?*"

Oh! You speak French?

"*Je fais. Nous avons passé nos étés à Marseille quand nous étions enfants,*" he responded just as fluently as me.

I do. We spent our summers in Marseille as children.

He took another sip of his drink as he looked off into the distance.

"Emma and I always wished the summer home had been in Paris instead, but I guess it was fine," he said, switching back over to English. "A bit dull, but what can you do?" Then he laughed at what he'd just said. "Hashtag *rich people problems*, am I right?"

Ollie looked utterly bewildered now, as he snapped his head back and forth between us like he was watching a tennis match. I'm sure he felt like he'd missed a major part of the conversation. I'd have to tell him later that he hadn't missed much.

"Right," I said in my French-accented English, trying not to let my sarcasm seep through.

Sam smiled at us for another brief second and then seemed to remember that we were all standing outside in the cold, and took a step back as he gestured for us to come inside.

"Welcome to Chateau Brasko," Sam said, closing the door behind us. "I hope you're ready for some fun."

Entry Seventeen

"If these walls could talk," Sam said as he walked through the grand foyer, gesturing sweepingly.

Then he turned back and winked at us.

"Well, if these walls could talk, let's be honest, we'd all be in a lot of trouble, wouldn't we?"

He laughed at his own joke, and Ollie and I both laughed as well, mostly because it would've been awkward if we hadn't.

"What magazine are you from again?" Sam asked as he led us down a long corridor lined with floor-to-ceiling windows. Little lights glowed beneath us as we walked, sparkling like stars under our feet. "Forgive me, our publicist, Bianca, must have forgotten to program this interview into our calendar. See, the girl's great at lining things up, but not so good at letting us know about it. Which, admittedly, might not be the best quality in a publicist, am I right? Maybe we should fire her. . . ."

I wanted to defend the girl that we'd thrown under the bus by creating this ruse, but I couldn't without risking our whole plan. Besides, if the publicist was fired now, it might be a blessing in disguise. Imagine the drama she'll have to deal with when the public finds out what the twins have been up to.

"We are from *French Fur* magazine," I supplied with a slight air of arrogance. "The premier animal magazine for the world's elite. We only cover the most *prominent* of society. And their pets, of course."

"Well, you've come to the right place," Sam said as he led us to a part of the house the size of a small auditorium. "I take it we qualify?"

I nearly dropped my facade completely as we were ushered into the room, and I saw how it was decorated.

It was like a museum.

For their dogs.

Inside were human-size statues of dog bones in one corner, dozens of miniature animal-print couches, tiny four-poster dog beds, and what I'm sure were solid gold food and water dishes placed atop a miniature oak doggy table.

And lining the walls were portraits of Lady Godiva and Titan. The animals had clearly sat for every single painting, a feat I'm not quite sure how they'd accomplished.

Uncle Scotty's entire house could've fit into their dog room, and here this was, completely devoted to two pampered dogs.

It was insane.

"A bit over-the-top, I know," Sam said sheepishly,

seeming to read my mind. "It started with just a few dog beds and toys, but then it turned into a whole room. And that's when we came up with the *Pet Palace Project*."

"I see," I said. And I did. I didn't really understand it—wasting all this decadence on a few dogs—but I could see what he was saying. At this point, they *needed* to expand. "Very . . . intriguing."

"So, what are we looking at here?" Sam asked, clapping his hands together like he was ready to get to work. "Are we talking a photo shoot? An in-depth feature. The cover?"

I was just about to answer when I felt the presence of someone behind me. There had been no footsteps. No ruffling of clothes. The person had been as quiet as a ninja. But I'd been doing this long enough to know when somebody had entered the room unannounced. It was a skill that had taken me a long time to hone, but had served me well.

So, when the person eventually spoke, it didn't make me jump. But Ollie did.

"Yes, I'd be very curious to hear what you have planned," a woman's voice said from behind me.

The three of us turned to see Sam's sister standing at the room's entrance, holding Lady Godiva in her arms and staring at us curiously. She was wearing a green dress with flowers sprinkled all over it. The sleeves were long and billowy, and on her tiny frame, it appeared like the dress was about to swallow her up.

"*Mademoiselle* Emma," I said, trying to make my smile appear real. "Well, don't you look lovely?"

She cocked her head to the side and surveyed me, the slightest of smiles playing on her lips. Then she began to walk across the room as the dress swirled along behind her. The whole thing felt very dream-like, and when I glanced over at Ollie, I could see he was caught up in the show, too.

"If I'd known you were coming, I would've dressed up. Funny that we're only hearing about this now."

"I was just saying we need to fire Bianca," Sam said as he plopped down into a nearby chair. "With the show starting to film in the next few days, we need someone who's on top of things around here."

"Agreed. It's not a good look to waste people's time," Emma said, joining her brother and taking a seat on the arm of his chair. She put Lady Godiva down on the ground and we all watched as the Pomeranian immediately ran over to a pink satin covered dog bed near a window and lay down. Emma turned her focus back on us and finally gave us what appeared to be a genuine smile. "So, please forgive us for being so clueless about this. Would you mind catching us up on what you'd like to do? I promise from now on, we'll be model subjects."

She was so breezy about it. Just like she'd been during the interview at the dog movie. And she seemed truly apologetic—even if she didn't really have a reason to be.

I decided my cover persona, Brigeet, would be annoyed but would ultimately give the twins a second chance. She would know better than anyone how difficult it was to find good help.

Plus, we needed to stay in their good graces—and on their property—if we were going to hunt down the exotic animals they were rumored to have.

"We would like to do an in-depth interview with the Brasko twins, culminating in a ten-page spread as well as the cover," I said in my French-American accent. "*French Fur* only covers society's most fabulous animal lovers. In the past we have interviewed Simon Cowell, Kristen Bell, Christian Miles . . ."

As I'd hoped, the twins seemed caught off guard at the mention of their alleged former client. I watched from behind my glasses as the two locked eyes, and Emma gripped the chair beneath her tightly. Sam crossed his legs and leaned back into the furniture before rubbing his neck absently.

Interesting. So, they *did* know Christian.

Their body language had made that abundantly clear. Both of them had displayed textbook signs of guilt or nervousness when I'd brought him up. But why? Had Christian been telling the truth when he'd fingered Sam to the FBI for the exotic animal traders? Or was there something else that tied him to the twins that would make them this tense? And lastly, was it just Sam running the exotic scam or was Emma in on it, too?

I decided to put on the pressure and see where we ended up.

114

"Wait—" I said as if the thought had just come to my mind. "You two know Christian, correct? I completely forgot. He's the one who told me about what it is you do."

"We know Simon Cowell, too," Sam said, trying to sound impressive while distancing himself from Christian. "Pre *Idol*, we all used to have game nights at his house."

"That was so thoughtful of Mr. Miles to *mention* us," Emma said, seeming lost in thought as she traced a flower along the fabric of her dress. "We all sort of run in the same circles—call it the Billionaire Boys club, if you will—but if I'm being honest, we didn't know each other *all* that well. What did he say about us? All good things, I hope."

You mean, did he spill that you two are just as sketchy as he was?

"Obviously, he holds you in high regard, otherwise we wouldn't be here," I said, implying that they had passed some invisible test of ours that deemed them worthy of being noticed.

If I hadn't been watching so closely, I may not have noticed the way their bodies relaxed at this.

"We'll have to thank Christian for the introduction next time we see him," Sam said, before realizing what he'd said. He immediately began to blush at his faux pas.

Emma cleared her throat and saved her brother from more embarrassment.

"Of course, that might be a long time from now, given

his current . . . predicament," she said, trying to be tactful in how she phrased it.

"Unfortunately, I suspect it will be," I said, trying to sound a bit annoyed by the whole thing. I turned around and began to walk the room, appearing to survey all the dog-inspired tchotchkes that made up the décor. "Christian was a good friend of mine. We've known each other for years. I thought it was a shame your country trapped him the way they did. Such a clever man deserves to be honored, not torn down."

"But he *did* break the law," Emma ventured carefully.

"In my country, that's just called being a business-man!" I said, throwing my arm in the air as if to brush Christian's indiscretions off. "But alas, we are not in France, we are here. And here, we have you!"

I rapped my hands together twice quickly.

"So, we shall get started?" I asked, not bothering to wait for them to recover from everything that had just been said. I wanted them a bit off-balance. It would make them agreeable and more likely to make mistakes. "Good. We would like you to be the subject of our comeback issue. It will be about the underdog of the moment. It will be about animal print. It will be about the Brasko Twins. It will be fabulous, no?"

Emma and Sam looked stunned, incapable of wrapping their heads around the ramblings of a crazy French editor. They looked at each other as I waited impatiently for them to react. In the end it was Sam who finally spoke.

"Well, we never really went anywhere," he said with a cocky smile. "So . . ."

"But you left the spotlight years ago, no? A scandal of some sort as I recall?" I asked, knowing I was poking the bear, but also believing it would get me what I wanted.

Sam frowned as Emma bit her lip.

"It doesn't matter," I said indifferently. "The important thing is that you seem to have picked yourself up once again. And now you are king and queen of this *jungle*?"

Another furtive look between the two.

"What exactly do you mean?" Sam asked. There was something in his eyes now. It wasn't anger, exactly. Or even fear. More like the look an animal gets when it's backed into a corner.

Fight or flight.

He was trying to figure out which to do.

Neither was going to get me what I wanted.

The only thing that would do that would be to build a relationship with them. Get them to trust me.

And that would take more time.

"We'd like to highlight everything that will be coming up in your new reality show, of course," I said finally.

I saw them both visibly relax and knew I'd said just the right thing to keep them from running. Or clamming up completely.

"My dears, I think it's going to put you back on top," I continued. "People will worship you again. And with an in-depth feature in *French Fur*, your standing with the rich and powerful will once again be solidified. With my help, we'll make the people go *wild* over you."

It was what they needed to hear.

They wanted it all back. The fame. The fortune. The power.

And I'd convinced them this was the way to get it.

Go me.

The twins seemed to confer in silence before turning to me.

"We're in," Emma said excitedly. "What do you need us to do."

Entry Eighteen

"I thought we were dead for sure," Ollie said.

We were talking over some details on the phone later that day and Ollie was still riding the high of our first meeting with the Brasko twins. He kept going over everything that had happened, as if I hadn't been there with him. It was actually kind of adorable.

There had been a time when I'd been new to it all too.

My mind started to drift to Dad, but I forced myself to refocus. There was no time for that at the moment. Right now, we had a heist to plan.

"Have I ever steered you wrong?" I asked Ollie as I folded up Brigeet's costume and placed it in a bag in my thieves trunk, along with all my other personas. "Now, where to go from here . . ."

We went over the details of what I'd proposed to Emma and Sam, point by point, so we were both on the same page. Since their doc crew would be starting to film in two days, we had just enough time to get everything together in order to pull it off.

We'd be there when they started to film and be privy to everything that happened behind the scenes. I'd explained that we needed to see their *entire* journey in order to relay their transformation to our readers in a real and honest way.

So, they'd given us unfettered access to their property and themselves.

Which was exactly what we needed in order to find out where they were hiding the animals.

"Okay, I think that about covers it," I said into the phone as I lay back on my bed, tired from all the excitement of the day.

"Frankie?" Ollie said just as I was about to hang up.

"Yeah, Ollie," I answered.

"I really think I could handle a few lines next time," he said confidently.

"Okay," I said, yawning. "Say, 'Frankie is the best thief in the whole world' with a French accent."

"Frankee ease thee best thief een the whole wold," he complied.

After a brief pause, I began to laugh loudly.

"What *was* that?" I answered, still cracking up.

"My French accent," Ollie said.

"That is not a French accent," I answered.

"It is!" he exclaimed. "I might not speak it fluently like you, but that was absolutely a French accent."

I snorted.

"Maybe keep working on it," I said, chuckling before hanging up.

There was a knock at my door and Uncle Scotty popped his head into my room.

"You watching a comedy show or something?" he asked.

"Something like that," I answered with a smile. Then I held up my phone. "Ollie."

Uncle Scotty nodded. "Ah, gotcha," he concluded. "Dinner will be here in ten."

"What are we having?" I asked as I ran my hand through my now short hair.

"Burgers," he answered, but then looked concerned. "Unless you suddenly became a vegetarian on me."

"*I haven't changed*, Uncle Scotty!" I yelled playfully. "I'm the same Frankie I've always been, I promise! I'm just a bit, you know, lighter in the hair department."

"If you say so," Uncle Scotty said, before disappearing again.

"I *do* say so," I said, turning the phone over and over in my hands.

I nearly jumped off the bed when it started to buzz.

I looked at the screen. It wasn't Ollie. His number would've popped up on the display. This was a number I didn't recognize. And it was from Colorado.

Did I know anyone in Colorado?

I considered sending it to voice mail, but my curiosity got the better of me, even though it was most likely just a telemarketing call.

"Hello? You've reached Domino's Pizza, how can I feed you today?" I asked, sounding like a typical teen at a dead-end job.

There was silence on the other line, which I attributed to the caller thinking they'd dialed the wrong number, and it made me want to start laughing.

"Frankie?" the voice came out with a strong Scottish accent.

Ugh. I hated telemarketing calls.

"Who's asking?" I asked, slightly annoyed.

"It's Angus, lass."

Angus? As in one of Dad and my former colleagues? The one I hadn't heard from in over two years?

"What's wrong, Angus?" I asked, suddenly filled with fear. Out-of-the-blue phone calls only happened when something was wrong, right? "I mean . . . how are you doing?"

Angus chuckled.

"Nothing's wrong," he answered. "Well, nothing's wrong with *me*. It's you I'm worried about."

I let the breath I'd been holding in out, along with my anxiety.

"I'm fine, Angus," I said, rolling my eyes even though he couldn't see me. "Why would you think something's wrong?"

"Yer dad told me what happened—"

Wait . . . *what*?

"You talked to Dad?" I asked, surprised by this.

We'd gone our separate ways from Angus after our last heist together. Not because Angus was a bad guy or anything—he and my dad had been friends for over a decade, and at one point, I'd been closer to him than I had to Uncle Scotty—but because Dad had had a kid he was trying to raise solo, and Angus simply had a different thieving style. In the end, we'd said our "goodbyes" and "good lucks" and moved on to the next job without him.

And I hadn't talked to him since.

Until now.

"Sure," Angus said. "I've phoned him a few times since he's been inside. Still the same old Tommy . . ."

"I don't know about that, but okay," I said, crossing my feet at the ankles angrily. As my dad's friend, I was sure Angus would take his side of the argument. And I didn't want to hear it.

"Well, look who's grown some sass!" he said, letting out a low whistle. "Yer dad told me you were pipin' mad. He feels bad, you know."

"He should. It was his fault," I said, knowing I sounded like a petulant child and hating it. "I mean, would *you* let him tell you what to do?"

There was a pause on Angus's end.

"Well, no," he answered slowly. "But to be fair, he isn't me daddy now is he?"

I smiled, only because I knew he couldn't see me do it.

"Lucky you," I said sarcastically.

Speaking like this, it felt like no time had passed. Like he'd always been around. Like I could talk to him as the real me.

"He said I should just be *normal*, Angus," I blurted out.

"Eeesh," Angus said whistling low. "That's rough."

"That's hypocritical," I added.

"True," Angus said. "But maybe he had his reasons, lass."

"Like what?" I asked, more heat in my voice than I'd intended.

Angus, to his credit, only answered softly.

"It can be hard where he is, lass. He's just tryin' to keep ye safe."

"By getting me to change who I am?" I asked him, still frustrated. "How can being *normal* possibly help me survive this place?"

"I imagine he thinks that if ye don't get into trouble, he can keep you from a similar fate," Angus said slowly.

"Maybe he should've started by taking that advice himself," I said, grumpily. "It's his fault I'm here in the first place!"

We both knew I didn't mean it. That I didn't *actually* blame Dad for ending up where he was.

"So, ye don't like livin' with yer uncle then?" he asked, sounding surprised.

I paused.

"I don't mind Uncle Scotty, actually," I said slowly. "It's all the rest I guess."

"So, what is it?" he asked, seeming genuinely curious.

Should I tell him the truth? Would he understand? Was there even any point?

"I'm kind of just . . . *lost*?" I started, wading in slowly, like entering into cold water. "I can feel the old me slipping away, Angus. Little by little. And I don't like it. I liked myself as *Frankie Lorde, International Thief.* I'm not really feeling *Frankie Lorde, Middle Schooler.* She's so . . . uninspiring."

"Now, that I disagree with," he cut in forcefully. "You might be in a rut right now, but the thing that makes you the *Infamous Frankie Lorde* will always be there in ye."

"I don't know," I said, not fully believing him.

"Yer dad mentioned ye pulled a job a few months back that helped a lot of people who needed it? That's nothing short of inspiring. Sounds like yer changin', but in a good way."

I hadn't thought of it that way before. That maybe I was changing, but for the *better*? My focus had been on others more than on myself since I'd moved here. But was that just me adapting to the change that was being forced on me by my uncle? Or was that me . . . growing up?

"I'm actually working a job now," I added carefully. "Well, we just started it, really. Can I tell you about it?"

I said this tentatively, not sure if he wanted to listen to some kid's amateur heist plan. But I'd been dying to talk to someone who knew about this stuff, and Dad hadn't exactly been receptive. Maybe Angus could be my sounding board.

"Are ye crazy?" he answered.

My stomach dropped.

"*Of course* I do," he finished.

I grinned and then flopped down onto my stomach on the bed and started to lay the whole plan out for him.

When I was done, he remained silent for just a moment before letting out a loud whoop.

"Yer really somethin', aren't ye," Angus said.

"You think it's good?" I asked, not realizing until now how much I wanted his approval.

"I think it's *great*," Angus answered, letting the word roll off his tongue. "I think the old Tommy Lorde would be proud of you."

I felt the tears begin to sting my eyes and my throat started getting tight. Then, I forced it all down. The last thing I wanted was to become a blubbering mess over the phone—to another thief!

"Thanks, Angus."

It was all I could get out without fully breaking down.

If he could hear it in my voice though, he didn't let on, and I really appreciated it.

"Ye know, lass," he said suddenly. "If yer really unhappy there, ye can always go on the road with me. I'm sure I could convince yer Dad to let ye."

This was the last thing I'd expected to hear him say, and for one of the first times in my life, I was at a loss for words.

The idea of heading back out there and being a thief

on the run again was certainly appealing. I missed traveling. I wouldn't miss going to school. But could I really just up and leave? Cut ties with Uncle Scotty and Ollie and disappear?

But it meant me being *me* again.

"I know, I know," Angus said, filling in the silence. "It's a big decision. And one ye don't have to make tonight."

"It's a really great offer, Angus," I said, not sure what to say. "Can I think about it for a bit? Get back to you when I've sorted things out?"

"Aye," he answered. "Tell ye what. I'm headed in yer direction in a few weeks. Got a job up in Quebec I have to do. What do ye say, I stop by and see ye in person. It can be either a quick visit or a pick-up. No pressure."

I let out a breath.

"That sounds good," I said, relieved I had some time to make my decision. "Thanks again, Angus."

"Yer always welcome, lass," he said, and I could tell by the way he said it that he meant it.

"Talk to you soon," I said before hanging up.

I sat there on my bed for a while, taking in what had just happened.

"Frankie!" Uncle Scotty's voice called out from downstairs, jolting me out of my head. "Burgers are here!"

I'd completely forgotten about dinner.

"Coming!" I yelled back, and stood up, looking around the room.

I hadn't had a place to call home for—I don't know how long.

And now I was thinking of giving it up?

I shook my head.

I wasn't going to make any decisions on an empty stomach. Choosing my path could come later.

After my burger and fries.

Entry Nineteen

"*Born to be* wild*!*"

Ollie sang the words off-key and loudly for about the hundredth time in the last half hour.

"It's getting old, Ollie," I said with a sigh as we walked down the paved road to the lion enclosure.

"Hey, I'm not the one who named the place after such a catchy tune," Ollie said.

"It was a clever choice," I admitted, looking around.

Ever since Kayla had mentioned the wild animal sanctuary during our conversation about exotics, I'd wanted to go to visit.

Not just because it had been ages since I'd been to anything like a zoo, but because I knew that it was going to be the best place for us to find out what we were getting into. So, we'd made the trip out of town to see it all for ourselves.

So far, it had not disappointed.

The lion quietly growled as we walked up, eyeing our every step to make sure we didn't get too close. I wanted to tell her to chill. We had *no intention* of getting up in her space.

It would've been impossible anyway because she was

currently lying down on an enormous rock looming high above a deep man-made moat. And even if she managed to cross the water, there was still another hard-core fence between her and us.

For now we were safe.

I think.

"Lions are just big cats," Ollie said, sounding like he was trying to convince himself of the fact. "So, they hate water, too, right? Which means my fears of that majestic beast swimming over here, scaling the fence and eating me for a kitty snack is just crazy . . . right?"

"I hope so," I said, only partly kidding. "When I looked this place up online, nothing came up about their animals eating the visitors. I'm assuming it would be bad for business."

"You think?" Ollie answered sarcastically.

"And here we have Sugar," said the tour guide, pointing at the lioness we were currently gawking at. "Sugar is a four-year-old African lion who came to the Born to Be Wild Exotic Animal Sanctuary by way of a rescue out in Florida."

At the sound of her name, the large lioness looked our way and yawned before turning her back to us again.

"That's not very polite, Sugar!" the guide, whose nametag read MICHAELA, right underneath the Born to Be Wild logo, scolded playfully. "These folks came from all over to see you!"

At that, Sugar turned her head once more, and gave us a roar that could only be described as bored.

I was convinced it was her way of letting us know she wasn't impressed by our presence.

"That a girl," Michaela said and pressed a button that dropped a treat down to the golden cat.

She licked it up with one swipe of her enormous tongue and then went back to ignoring us.

"Now, I know Sugar looks cute and all—she primped all morning for you guys—but there's a reason there are so many obstacles between that sweet cat and us," Michaela said. "First off, even though she's only four, Sugar weighs in at a whopping two hundred seventy pounds. Second, the fastest human in the world can run twenty-eight miles per hour. A lion can get up to nearly twice that. Third, and most important, she's all muscle and claws. Oh, and teeth."

"Yeah, don't want to forget those," Ollie muttered.

"That's why we all need to be so careful when we're around exotic animals like Sugar," Michaela said. "As a predator, lions and other big cats are hardwired to hunt and prey on those weaker than them. And I hate to break it to you, but you are *all* weaker than Sugar. Yeah, even you, beefcake."

This drew a few laughs from the families gathered around us, but I was already raising my hand.

"Yes," Michaela said, pointing to me. "Narwhal girl."

I blinked and glanced behind me to see who she had called on.

Then Ollie elbowed me in the side. "That's you," he

hissed, pointing not so subtly at what was on my shirt.

I looked down and read the print. Even upside down, I knew what it said.

Save the Narwhals (They're the unicorns of the sea.)

"Right," I said, pulling my jacket closed out of embarrassment. Then I cleared my throat and spoke up. "Um, you said that Sugar was rescued in Florida. Is that how you get most of your animals?"

"Good question, Narwhal," Michaela began. Slowly, everyone turned back to our guide and eventually forgot all about me. And my shirt.

"Ha, ha, ha, ha," Ollie laughed quietly. "Narwhal girl. That's *so* going to be your new nickname."

"Only if you want me to kick your butt," I retorted. "You know I took krav maga for a few years when we were in Israel. I can disarm a person as fast as I can steal your wallet."

Ollie stopped laughing.

"So, some of our animals are born here in captivity," Michaela said, answering my question. "Which means we get to raise them from when they're just this big."

She held up her hands to show a space about the size of a volleyball.

"So, probably smaller than when any of you were first born," Michaela added to give some context.

I could hear a few *awww*s break out around us and then a woman shouted, "Can we pet the babies later?"

Michaela shook her head.

"Sorry, like I said before," she answered. "They're cute, but deadly. If you want to leave here with all your limbs, can I suggest you visit the zoo gift shop and snag a snuggly stuffie that won't bite?"

A few more laughs around me.

Was she practicing her standup routine or something?

I sighed and raised my hand again. This time, I didn't wait for Michaela call on me.

"And where do you get the rest of your animals?" I asked.

"Ah, yes," Michaela answered. "It's true, most of our exotic animals are rescued all around the country. Usually from people who owned them privately and for whatever reason, can't anymore."

"Wait, regular people keep animals like Sugar . . . as pets?" I made it sound like the idea was preposterous, even though I knew it was true.

"Another great question," Michaela said, sounding like she meant it. "The truth is, there are more captive tigers in the US than there are in the wild, *in the whole world*. And part of that is because some people think it would be cool to own a lion or a tiger or a monkey, and don't think of the consequences—like how expensive it is to feed them, the kinds of enclosures you need to keep a fully grown big cat from harming anyone."

"These people are so clueless that around sixty percent of exotics that end up at rescues are abandoned pets," Michaela said. "But those are the lucky ones, because it's estimated that ninety percent of wild animals that are kept as pets die within the first two years of captivity. This can be because of ignorance, neglect, a lack of resources—and yes, euthanizing."

"They kill them?" an older man said off to my right. "Geez."

I watched another woman shudder and then sneak a sad look over at Sugar.

Michaela saw this too, and must have decided the topic was a little too depressing for her upbeat adventure.

"Well, why don't we move on to the tigers!" she said, pointing us in the direction of the next exhibit.

I was bummed to move on, because I'd barely skimmed the top of the information I'd wanted from Michaela. But it wasn't like I could force her to stop and give me a solo lesson on the ins and outs of exotic animal life.

Ollie and I began to follow the rest of the group and I gave one last lingering look back at Sugar.

"Narwhal!" a voice called out.

I looked up to see Michaela moving through the group and hurrying over to us.

"Hey," she said as she landed in front of me. She pushed her glasses up onto her face and then tightened her ponytail.

"Lane," I said, offering her my middle name instead of the nickname she'd given me.

"Right," she said with a smile. "Sometimes it's just easier to refer to guests by what they're wearing."

134

"It's cool," I said, though I hoped to never hear myself referred to as Narwhal ever again.

"So, Lane," she started again. "I was vibing that you've got a lot of questions about big cats."

"I do," I said, nodding. "But I know you have a whole script to stick to. . . ."

I gestured at the people who were milling around us.

"Well, why don't we talk while we walk to the tigers? What do you wanna know?"

"Oh," I said, surprised by the gift I'd just been given.

My own personal expert? Yes, please.

"Awesome," I said, trying to organize my thoughts quickly. "Uh, okay. I guess I'm sort of interested in learning more about the exotic animal trade?"

Michaela raised an eyebrow as we walked.

"This for a school project or something?" she asked, practically handing me my cover.

"Yeah," I said easily.

"Over the holiday break?" she continued.

Ollie and I nodded.

"Yeesh," she said. "That sucks."

"You have no idea," I answered.

"So, how can I help you get an *A* on this project?" she asked finally.

"Well, isn't it true that some people think that if you raise a big cat from a cub that they won't, um . . . *attack* you later? Like, they'll basically be like a really big house cat?"

"People *do* think that, Lane, but it's also why so many

of them end up abandoned," Michaela answered. "Let me set the scene for you: A tiger cub is just over two pounds when it's born. Super cute, especially when you get to feed them out of a baby bottle. At that size, they're totally manageable."

Michaela lifted up her phone and showed me a picture of herself holding a brand-new tiger cub.

"So stinking cute, right?" Michaela said. Then she added, "The tiger, I meant. Not me."

Ollie and I nodded. The cat *was* just about the cutest thing I'd ever seen. It made me almost forget it was a dangerous, wild animal.

"So, out the gate they're small and cute, but by just three months old, the tiger baby is officially dangerous," Michaela said, showing us another picture of herself with the same tiger a few months later.

It was definitely bigger—about thirty pounds bigger. His paws were the size of my hands, and his claws were like full-blown knives.

"At this age, a tiger cub is already big enough to push down an adult human. And even its play bites can do damage," Michaela said.

She stopped walking and rolled up the sleeve of her shirt. Underneath was a long, white scar down the length of her arm. Michaela saw me eyeing the injury and held it out.

"Go ahead," she said. "You can touch it."

I reached out and felt the jagged scar. The skin there

was ultra smooth, like when ice cream melts and then hardens back up. Up close, I could see all the little dots where the wound had been held closed by staples or stitches. Most people might've been grossed out by a scar like that, but I kind of liked it.

It was like a strange badge of honor.

And I had a feeling Michaela felt the same way.

"Freaky, huh?" she said, a little twinkle in her eye.

"It's rad," I agreed.

Ollie looked between the two of us.

"You two are super weird," he stated bluntly. "No offense, but nothing's so *rad* that I'd let a tiger claw me."

"And that's my official stance, too," Michaela said seriously. "It took thirty-six stitches to close this baby up. And Sweet Pea was only playing around. She didn't even *mean* to do it. Imagine if it had been on purpose."

"Please don't make me imagine it," Ollie said, looking queasy.

"Fair enough," she said. "Anyways, just because a person raises a cub, doesn't mean the animal loses their natural instincts. Those stick around long after they've grown."

"So then why are people allowed to own exotics in the first place?" I asked.

"That's a complicated question with an even more complicated answer," she said. "Right now, there are no federal laws in place banning exotic animal ownership in general. However, over a dozen states have banned

137

private possession, another dozen require a license or permit to own them, and about seven states have a partial ban."

"Where does Connecticut fall in there?" Ollie asked.

"It's illegal to have a tiger as a pet if you're simply Joe Schmo here in Connecticut," Michaela said. "You've gotta have a zoo or sanctuary/rescue license."

"Gotcha," I said, filing that away.

"So, if it's illegal in a lot of places, then why are there still so many animals out there?" Ollie asked her.

"Supply and demand," Michaela answered with a shrug. "It's not that expensive to buy any kind of animal you want over the Internet. You can bring home a monkey for a few thousand bucks. And tigers are even cheaper. You can get one of them for under $300. That's less than one of those fancy show dogs."

"Geez," Ollie said, shaking his head.

"And costs are low because it's such a huge industry," Michaela continued. "The illegal business of selling exotic animals is second only to drugs in the US—bringing in around ten billion dollars annually. And yet, you're *way* more likely to get jail time for smuggling drugs than say, a sloth, into the country."

"That's messed up," Ollie said.

"It's totally messed up," Michaela agreed.

"Thank *you*," I told her. "I'm definitely gonna get an A on this one. I know you're busy. . . ."

"Nah, I love talking about this stuff!" Michaela said.

"It's why I'm here."

Then she winked and walked back to the front of our group before beginning to tell the group everything she knew about tigers.

"Well, that was . . . eye-opening," I said.

"That was terrifying," Ollie said, shuddering. "That scar. So. Gross."

"Are you kidding?" I exclaimed. "That was epic."

Ollie shook his head. "You're nuts," he said. "I can't believe *you're* my mentor."

"I don't have to be, you know," I said casually.

Ollie snorted. "Because there are so many thieves out there willing to take on a kid like me?" he said sarcastically. "I had to practically *force* you to do it."

"True," I agreed. "Maybe you should quit while you're ahead."

Ollie stopped walking.

"Hold up," he said, waving his finger in my face grandly. "What are you talking about?"

I sighed.

I'd wanted to tell Ollie about my talk with Angus almost as soon as we'd had it, but for some reason I'd been holding back. At first, I told myself it was because I didn't want to freak him out. But the truth was, I wanted to figure out how I felt first.

The only problem was: I still had no idea what I wanted to do.

"Soooo," I started, trying to keep my voice light and

airy. "One of Dad and my old partners in the 'industry' got in touch."

Ollie's eyes grew big.

"Is there a job?" he asked, sounding excited by the prospect.

"Not exactly," I said slowly.

Ollie's face fell.

"Okay," he said. "Well, then, what?"

"I told him how I was feeling about being stuck here, and he kind of, sort of, may have invited me to go on the road with him?" I said, squishing up my face until his became a blur.

"Oh."

I opened one of my eyes and saw that Ollie was focused straight ahead. He looked like he was thinking and I gave him the time to get his thoughts in order.

"Are you going?" Ollie asked. I could tell he was holding back any emotion he was currently feeling, and felt bad that he was keeping that side of himself from me.

I kicked at a rock.

"I don't know," I admitted. "I told him I'd think about it. He's going to come through town in a few weeks and I'm supposed to give him my decision then."

Ollie nodded.

"Can I ask you why?" Ollie said quietly. "Like, is it really so awful for you being here?"

I hadn't expected this question. At least not in the way he'd asked it. And to his credit, it was a fair one. But how could I explain it in a way that wouldn't hurt Ollie's feelings?

"Being here—I just feel *stuck*, Ollie," I said, trying to choose my words carefully. "Until I got here, life felt so big, so open. Like I could go anywhere and do anything. Now I feel like I'm in a—"

"Cage?" Ollie finished for me.

I let out a breath.

"Yeah."

Ollie was silent again as he mulled this over.

"There's something else, too," I added tentatively. "It's hard to explain, but I feel less like myself here? Like I can't be the real me. Or maybe like the old me is slipping away? I don't know if I can fulfill my destiny living here in Greenwich. Being restrained like this. I'm afraid I'll never make it out."

Ollie turned to me, a pained look on his face.

"I actually know how you feel, Frankie," he said with a sigh. But when his gaze finally met mine, it was with a tremendous amount of guilt. "There's something I have to show you."

And then he took my hand and led me away.

Entry Twenty

"I haven't been a hundred percent truthful with you, Frankie."

My stomach sunk.

It *had* to be bad if Ollie had kept it from me. Because, let's be honest: it's not like Ollie held much inside.

And *I* was his best friend.

What could he possibly have hidden from me?

"Don't tell me you were lying when you said I looked skinny in these pants," I said, mock-horrified.

When he didn't break out laughing at my joke, I took a breath.

"Okay, so what did you do then?" I asked my drama queen of a friend.

"I didn't really *do* anything," he said deliberately. "And maybe it's not really *that* big of a deal."

"I'm sure it isn't," I answered, glancing out the window absently. I wasn't even sure where we were going. Ollie had ordered us an Uber on his parents' account before we'd left the rescue, telling me our destination was a surprise.

And I hadn't pushed him on it even though I loathed surprises.

I think it shows just how much I've grown since moving here.

"What part of town is this?" I asked as we pulled off onto a private road and I started to see houses that were at least three times the size of Uncle Scotty's.

"Byram," Ollie answered.

"Why are we here?" I asked, the flutters of curiousity starting to creep in.

I glanced out my window and saw that we were driving along the beach now. It was the first time I'd seen a body of water since moving to Greenwich and I got excited.

I always loved the beach. Dad and I would seek them out anywhere we went on our adventures. I'd even learned to surf in Hawaii one summer. I missed the way the sound of the waves drowned out all the noise in your head.

I could've used that living here.

We pulled up to a house that looked like it belonged on Cape Cod. Standing three stories tall, the mansion—because let's be honest, that's what it was—had a big red door in the middle, with two large windows flanking either side of it. The boxlike windows continued along the rest of the facade like freckles on a face. On one side of the house was a tall, cylindrical structure, sort of like a lighthouse, but almost completely glass. Large, steep roofs were held up with strategically placed white pillars, giving the place an even grander feel.

The place was opulent for sure, but somehow it still managed to give off an aura of quaintness.

Ollie still hadn't answered my question from before, and I turned back to face him.

"Ollie, who lives here?" I asked him again.

The car stopped and Ollie paused a second, purposely not looking over at me, and then opened his door.

"I do."

Entry Twenty-One

"You live here."

I said it like I didn't believe it. Because it was unbelievable.

Ollie just nodded.

"But—" I said, not sure what to say next. I shook my head. "I don't get it, Ollie."

"Let me show you," Ollie said carefully. "And then maybe it'll make more sense."

He started to walk up to the house so I followed.

Ollie pulled up a panel to the right of the door that was practically hidden since it blended in with the house, and then keyed in a few buttons. He didn't bother trying to shield the code from me, which I took as a sign that he definitely trusted me not to rob him later.

And I wouldn't. I promise.

"Mama!" Ollie called out as we walked into the massive foyer. "Papa, I'm home!"

There was no immediate answer, but Ollie acted like this was normal. He sat down on a nearby bench and took off his shoes. Then he motioned for me to do the same.

"Mom is crazy about dirt in the house," he explained with a shrug. He sounded almost embarrassed, but still held his hand out to take the shoes that I'd slipped off my feet.

Once I was barefoot, we walked between a set of pillars that signaled the end of the foyer and continued on into an even larger entryway.

Yes, there was a foyer *and* an entryway. Where was I?

As we walked further inside, I looked up in awe to see that the ceiling was three stories high, and had a five-foot-wide crystal chandelier hanging from the middle. There were dual black staircases that split the room and led to the floor above. Everything else was a pristine white, with the exception of the dozens of enormous hand-painted portraits that hung on each side of the room like a museum.

"Wow," I said, not able to stop myself as I looked around.

"I know," Ollie said with a sigh.

Each picture was around five feet in length and consisted of a different member of Ollie's family. Hand-painted in muted colors, each person was posed stiffly and seriously, like the ones displayed in royal families' homes. Or haunted houses.

There were old people, and then even older people, as well as kids and babies all featured on the walls. And there, in the middle of it all, was Ollie. He sat ramrod straight in a chair that I swear could've been in *Game of Thrones*. He was holding a white fluffy cat in his lap, appearing like he was midpet. In the photo, he wore a frown.

I looked over at him and saw the same frown on his face now.

"That's you," I said in shock.

"Yeah," he said.

"With a cat in your lap," I continued.

"Now can you see why I'm not a fan?" Ollie muttered. "My mom forced me to hold that stupid cat for nine hours. It wasn't even our cat. And it peed on my McQueen."

I stifled a laugh.

"Come on," Ollie said, clearly still not happy about the experience.

I trailed behind him as we made our way through the room toward the back, and noticed how all of Ollie's family members' portraits seemed to follow us creepily as we went.

"Does it sort of look like—" I began.

"Like their eyes are following us?" Ollie finished for me. "Yep."

"Okay," I said, and just kept walking.

As we continued through the entryway, past the staircases and into the room at the back of the house, I began to hear sounds. More specifically, the sound of people talking.

Loudly.

And animatedly.

"They can't always hear me from back here," Ollie explained as we got closer.

I was about to ask who, when we stepped into a large and open kitchen. It was the thing of chefs, with nearly two of everything. Two ranges, two ovens, two fridges—one was clear and just for drinks—and a massive island in the middle.

An island, which was completely covered with plates of food.

Beyond the island was an equally large dining area with a grand, twelve-person table in the middle, as well as a little breakfast nook that looked like it could seat six.

A cozy fireplace sat in the middle of the far wall and had already been fired up with the gas it took to run it. On the other side of that were a few couches, an oversized ottoman, and a flat-screen TV.

There was a lot going on in here.

And not just in the way of furniture.

Because we'd just walked into a dinner that was obviously already in full swing.

A woman around the same age as Uncle Scotty was standing nearby and I watched as she piled her plate high with food and then turned to grab some tortillas. It was midgrab that she saw us.

"*Aye, Sobrino!*" she said, holding her hand to her chest in surprise. "Don't sneak up on me like that!"

"I called out when I walked in the front, Auntie," Ollie said. "Nobody responded."

"Well, don't just lurk! You made it for dinner—come in and grab a plate," she said, motioning us over. Then she turned her head over her shoulder and yelled to everyone, "Oliver's home! And he's brought a *girl*!"

"Oliver's got a girlfriend, Oliver's got a girlfriend!" a little boy around the age of six said over and over again from the nook in the corner.

A woman disentangled herself from the group of grazers and came right up to us, taking both of my hands in hers before leaning in and giving me a kiss on my cheek.

It was sloppy and she nearly smothered me when she stuck my face into her chest. But it was warm and genuine.

"So wonderful to meet you . . . ," she started.

"Frankie," I supplied with a smile.

She pulled back, holding my arms out and looked at me.

"You're too skinny," she said. "Oliver, your girlfriend needs to eat."

"Maaaammmaaaa," Ollie whined quietly. "She's *not* my girlfriend. She's just my *friend*. And you can't say things like that to people."

"What?" Ollie's mom asked, looking confused. "But it's true."

"But it's *rude*," Ollie pointed out.

"It's okay," I said politely.

"See, Oliver?" his mom argued. "It's not *rude*. Rude would be telling her she'd look so much more feminine if she grew out her hair."

"Mom!" Ollie yelled, his cheeks burning red.

"Lucia, *novia*, leave the girl alone," an older man said appearing from behind us. Though Ollie was practically the spitting image of his mom, all the way down to her roundness and attitude, I knew right away that the man was Ollie's dad.

There was something about his eyes.

They were kind but also there was so much excitement there. A joy of life that was hard to find in people these days.

But Ollie's dad had it. And Ollie did too.

"I'm not doing anything!" Ollie's mom exclaimed, raising her hands defensively. "Just getting to know Ollie's girlfriend here."

"And giving her some unsolicited advice at the same time?" Ollie's dad added, flashing me a friendly smile. "Hello, *amiga*. I am Oliver's father."

I reached out and shook his hand.

"Well, maybe if more people listened to my *unsolicited advice*, the world wouldn't be quite so loco, Hugo," Lucia argued. "Ever think of that?"

"It's all I think about, *amor*," Ollie's dad said, and winked at us before steering his wife to a seat at the table.

"This is why we hang out at your house," Ollie muttered as he handed me a plate and began to fill his own.

"I don't know why," I said with a laugh. "This is incredible."

Ollie looked at me like I had two heads.

"Really!" I insisted. "All this energy and excitement.

It's nice to be a part of it. I grew up with it being just Dad and me. And now it's just Uncle Scotty and me. I mean, it's fine. I like being on my own. But sometimes I wonder what it would be like to have a big family."

"Um, *chaotic*," Ollie offered. "Annoying. Loud."

I laughed again.

"It's not that bad," I said, following him to the table and sitting down in an empty seat. I quickly texted Scotty to let him know I wouldn't be home for dinner, but that I was fine.

"What is that you're wearing, Oliver?" the man sitting next to his aunt asked while shoveling food into his mouth.

Ollie looked down.

"Um, a shirt," he replied.

"But it's all . . . ." His uncle gestured wildly to the design on the button-down. "Flowery."

Ollie sighed loudly.

"Yes," Ollie said plainly. "It *does* have flowers on it."

I had a feeling this was a conversation they had on the regular.

"Why do you have to dress all fancy all of the time? Why don't you wear things like Nike or Abercrombie like the other kids?"

Before Ollie could answer—or lose his cool—I jumped in.

"Obviously, Ollie needs clothes as fabulous as he is," I countered, giving him a supportive grin.

"You live in *Greenwich*, though," his uncle said. "Who are you trying to be fabulous for?"

I could see Ollie tense up beside me and I lightly brushed my shoulder against his in a show of solidarity.

As everyone finished their meals, they began to get up and say their goodbyes.

"See you *mañana*," Ollie's aunt said, gathering up the three boys and girl who'd been sitting in the booth table. "I'll come round eight to pick up Papa for his appointment."

Ollie's mom nodded.

Then, instead of heading in the direction of the front door, Ollie's aunt, uncle, and cousins piled out the sliding doors leading to the backyard. I watched in confusion as they walked around the large pool and then entered a smaller house about a hundred feet away from the main house.

"My aunt and uncle live in the guest house," Ollie explained, following my gaze. "And my grandparents live in their own section of this house on the first floor. They have their own little kitchen and everything."

"It's nice you're all so close," I said.

"A little *too* close sometimes," Ollie answered, still smarting about his uncle's comments from earlier.

"Most of the time when families have money, they grow apart. Or fight over it," I said.

"Oh, don't get it twisted," Ollie answered, as his mom and dad began to put away the leftover food. "The *Santiagos* don't have money."

I looked around the room slowly.

"Um, I would beg to differ," I countered.

"I mean, we don't *come* from money. We hit the lottery, Frankie."

"You are pretty fortunate—" I said.

"No," he cut in. "We *literally* won the lottery. I'm talking, my dad buying lotto tickets for thirty-seven years and finally hitting the jackpot rich."

My eyes widened.

"No way!" I exclaimed, fascinated by what he was saying.

I'd never met anyone in real life who'd won the lotto. I'd even questioned whether the whole thing was a hoax. But now here was Ollie and his family.

Rich overnight.

Ollie nodded.

"BTL—Before the Lotto—my mom cleaned other people's houses for a living and my dad was the head groundskeeper at an estate in the area. When we won, my folks quit their jobs, moved us to this house, brought along my grandparents, and aunt and uncle and their kids, and we all moved in here together."

"Okay. So, why wouldn't you want to tell me about this, Ollie?" I asked, confused. "Did you think I'd look at you differently?"

And then an upsetting thought popped into my mind again.

"Or did you think I'd rob you?"

I hated the thought that Ollie would worry I'd steal from him and his family. I thought he knew that now I only went after those who didn't deserve their wealth in the first place.

Ollie snorted.

"Please," he said. "We might have this great, big house, but it's not like we have anything in it for you to steal. Except for those creepy family portraits out there, which you're totally welcome to, I might add."

"No thanks," I said, shuddering. "If you weren't afraid I'd rob you and you didn't think I'd judge, then why wouldn't you tell me who you really are?"

"That's the thing . . . *this*," he said, gesturing widely around the room. "This isn't me. We may have money but we're not rich."

"I don't get it," I said, shaking my head.

"Nothing about us changed when we got the money. Yes, we moved. But we don't have a maid or housekeeper or chef to cater to our every whim. My mom doesn't believe in letting other people clean her house. Ironic, but she's always like, 'We can clean our own house, thank you very much.' So we do.

"Dad bought a piece of land nearby and turned it into a sort of community park where people can plant stuff. He's out there every day, breaking his back to keep things looking good for all the strangers who come through. He says it gives him purpose. I think it gives him back problems."

"So, you're *mad* that . . . you *have* money?" I asked, still not getting it. "But you don't get to spend it?"

"No," Ollie said, sounding frustrated. "I don't want people to know we have money, because they'll look at me like we have money, when in reality, we live our lives like we don't. Get it?"

"Uh," I said, starting to understand what he was trying to say. "I *think* so."

"All this money, and *nothing's* changed," he said. "I still live in this tiny little town, surrounded by people who think I'm weird and treat me differently because of the way I look. I have dreams of being a famous actor, but I still haven't gone on a single audition. I have all the money in the world, but I can't use it to become the person I know I'm meant to be."

"Awww, Ollie," I said, leaning over to hug him.

"I'm not saying this to make you feel bad for me," Ollie answered, shrugging me off. "I know I'm privileged. I know these are just rich people problems. But I wanted to show you that I understand being stuck in a place that's too small for you. That wants you to be someone you're not, so you can fit into a mold they've constructed."

Ollie's voice was imploring now and his eyes showed more emotion than his voice could convey. My happy-go-lucky Ollie felt just as caged in as I did. And I was only discovering that now.

"So, I'm asking you, as my best friend, *please* don't leave me here alone," he asked seriously. "I know you're bigger than this place. I know you feel stuck, because I do too. Just, please, for now, stay. And I promise, as soon as it's the right time, you will get out."

"How can you know that, Ollie?" I asked quietly.

He paused before putting his hand on my arm.

"Because I'll be going with you."

Entry Twenty-Two

The guards had looked at us suspiciously until we showed them our credentials.

Then they let us in through the gate, handed us the keys to our own golf cart and waved us off.

"These things are like golden tickets," Ollie said as he rode shotgun in the cart. "Or all-access passes that get us backstage at a Jonas Brothers concert."

I raised an eyebrow.

"These are better than a Jonas Brothers concert," I said, making a face.

"I guess that's a matter of opinion," Ollie said, the wind whipping his shaggy wig around his face. I'd hated the hairpiece when I'd first seen it, but it had grown on me. Especially because Ollie looked nothing like himself in it. And that was sort of the point of our disguises.

"But it can't be this easy, can it?" Ollie asked, gesturing around.

"When you lay a strong enough foundation, the rest builds itself," I said, steering us along the long driveway toward the Brasko estate.

When we made it up to the main house, I parked our

cart and we got out, gathered our things, and made our way inside.

Nobody came to greet us.

That's not to say there was nobody there.

It was actually quite the opposite.

A couple dozen people milled around just inside the house, busily setting up lights, taping down wires, and strategically placing microphones around each room.

Nobody paid attention to the French woman dressed in a chic, princess-style jacket with two rows of buttons splitting the middle of her chest. I'd admired the coat while we were on a job once. I loved the way that it was fitted at the top, and then how the slippery black material billowed out like a dress from there.

It wasn't until after I'd stolen it from the countess that I'd found out the frock was worth about $10,000.

I didn't care.

It could've cost a dollar and I still would've kept it.

Because I actually liked it. It was chic and classy and could work with so many different personas. It made me feel fancy. Like I wasn't just a common thief looking to steal a few bucks.

Besides, it was just smart to have a few nice things in your repertoire.

I brushed my own brown wig out of my face and then grumbled in annoyance as it fell back down over my eyes. It was the look I was going for: fine but unstyled. It was meant to blend in while my clothes stood out. I topped it all off with another pair of ridiculously oversized sunglasses. The frames were so big, they nearly took up my whole face.

This was the idea, since it made it even more difficult to get a good look at my face and features, and made it almost impossible for anyone to describe me later.

We walked past all the people scurrying around, stepping over cables as we went. Ollie teetered along behind me, holding a bunch of bags while I held only my small clutch.

I knew that Ollie was sweating by now. He broke out in a sweat on a cold day while standing still, so in here, under the already hot lights, carrying all our stuff—as an assistant would—he had to be soaked.

Luckily he was wearing his own pair of black skinny jeans and a fitted, black Versace sweater with a swirly gold print decorating the front, so you couldn't see if he was soaking through them. On his face was a pair of oversized gold glasses. The whole look was over-the-top for sure, but I had a feeling nobody would be paying much attention to us today.

Because today was all about Emma and Sam.

It was officially the first day of filming their reality show, and everyone seemed on edge. Or at the very least, distracted. Which was good.

I could work with distracted.

We followed the line of crew members through room after room until we finally found the twins. When we breezed through the door, they were both sitting in makeup chairs, lounging with drinks and magazines, as a group of people worked on them. I looked around and wondered if the glam room had always been there or if they'd built it especially for this.

Now that they were going to be filmed 24/7, I guess it made sense that they would need to be camera-ready. Wouldn't want to be shiny when we're being reintroduced to the world, now would we?

"Vous voilà deux," I said, sashaying over and standing in between them so they could both see me in their mirrors. *"Bonjour, mes chers. Êtes-vous prêt pour la journée?"*

There you two are! Good morning, my dears. Are you ready for the day?

"Oui!" Emma gushed, wiggling her toes in excitement. "Oh, Brigeet, can you believe this is all happening? This morning I woke up before it was even light out and just watched the sun rise. Have you ever watched the sun rise? And not, like, when you're heading home from the club and the sun happens to be coming up while you're half asleep in the back of a town car. I mean, like, waking up and bathing in the light of a new day!"

Emma finally took a breath and looked at me expectantly for a response. I quickly caught up with her rambling and brushed my hair away from my face absently.

"Oui. I've had the fortune of witnessing a sunrise or two in my time," I said in my French-American accent.

"I think I'd rather watch the sun set," Sam chimed in, taking a sip from his disgusting-looking green juice drink and giving one of the young makeup artists a wink. "More romantic, am I right?"

The girl gave him a flustered smile before starting to paint Emma's toenails.

A lanky, tall, and disheveled-looking guy walked into the room, hoodie pulled up over his head, hands in his pockets. I instantly took him for an intern. Or some assistant of the assistant.

I certainly wouldn't have pegged him as the one in charge.

"And how are you guys doing?" he asked, his voice sounding like a parent talking to a child. Sickly sweet but tentative, like at any moment the kid could blow.

I had to appreciate his foresight.

"Fabulous," Emma said, applying a layer of gloss to her lips while staring in the mirror. "Just finishing up."

"Oh," the guy said, looking utterly surprised. "That's great! Because all the cameras are up and ready to go. And the construction crew have been at the site waiting for you to arrive and kick off the project. So . . ."

Emma reached over to Sam and squeezed his arm excitedly.

"Awesome," Sam said, pointing out a section of his hair to the stylist and then closing his eyes so she could spray it with more hairspray.

"So, we should be done here in about, oh . . ." Emma

looked around the room, seeming to make a list in her head. "Maybe forty-five minutes? Definitely in an hour."

"Oh," the director said, deflating in front of our eyes. "Um, I guess I'll go to tell everyone to hang tight, then."

"Thanks, love," Emma said cheerfully.

As the guy turned to walk away, Emma suddenly sat up straight in her chair, sending the girl painting her nails to the ground as she followed her foot.

"Oh, Derek, wait!" she said. "I'm so rude, forgive me."

A relieved look washed over Derek's face as he turned back around to look at her.

"Yeah?" he asked hopefully.

"I just wanted to introduce you to Brigeet and her assistant," she turned to me, searching. "What's his name again? Never mind, it doesn't matter. They're from *French Fur* magazine and are here to do feature on us and the *Pet Palace Project*. You'll give them whatever they need, yeah?"

Derek shriveled up again but took a step toward me and held out his hand.

"Hey. I'm Derek. The director of this whole . . . thing," he said unenthusiastically. He gave me a curt smile and then raised his eyes back up to Emma and Sam. "So, thirty minutes then?"

He asked this with hope in his voice.

"Somewhere around there," Emma answered non-committally.

"Great," Derek, the director, muttered before slinking out of the room.

162

I thought about telling Emma that if she didn't want to be destroyed by the editors on the show, she should probably start treating the crew a little better, but then I remembered I didn't care about Emma and Sam.

I was here for another reason completely.

"We will let you two finish up here," I said, and motioned to Ollie that we were leaving.

"You don't want to start the interviews now?" Emma asked, frowning.

"I thought you would like to use this time to collect yourselves before your every thought and move is captured on the moving picture, no?" I said, trying to think of an excuse to get out of there without raising suspicion.

Emma stared at me blankly for a minute and I grew weary. Ollie and I needed some time to roam around the estate and try to find the exotics. We weren't going to be able to do that from here.

Finally, Emma's face broke out into a smile.

"Of course," she said, nodding. "That's an excellent idea. Maybe I'll do a little meditation and center myself with some breath work."

She reached forward and grabbed a few cucumber slices and placed them over her eyes before relaxing back into her chair.

I had a feeling she was about to take a nap instead of meditate, but I wasn't about to stop her. As long as her eyes were closed and she wasn't focused on what we were up to, I didn't care.

"Cool," Sam said, chugging the rest of his drink and hopping down from his chair. "I'm gonna go do some push-ups. I want to look jacked when we start filming."

He leaned over the stylist to grab his phone, grazing her body as he did it. After giving her a loaded look, he straightened back up before walking toward the door.

"I'll be in the gym if anyone wants to watch me work out," he offered to no one in particular.

No thank you.

There's somewhere else we needed to be.

Entry Twenty-Three

They weren't anywhere.

Ollie and I spent an hour driving around on that golf cart looking for the exotics and came up with nothing. The grounds were so vast, and at times hilly and so thick with trees, that they could've been hidden anywhere.

To keep suspicions low, we limited our search to about an hour, before heading back to the main house to watch the twins oversee the construction that had begun less than a hundred feet from their back door. While they filmed, we took the time to learn more about them.

Like, how Emma had two hundred pairs of heels in her closet, displayed in sections by color, yet she preferred to wear flats. Or that Sam played six different instruments and had a whole room downstairs set up with equipment just so he and his friends could have jam sessions.

Sometimes I liked them more after learning these fun little facts. Sometimes I was left even more motivated to destroy them. It seemed to change hourly.

When everyone broke for lunch, Ollie and I headed out again, driving on the other side of the property this time.

And still, there was nothing. No animals. No cages. No signs of wildlife anywhere.

The next few days were a blur of splitting our time between The Farm and our volunteer work there, and conducting our fake interviews with Emma and Sam when they weren't filming.

Fake or not, the interviews turned out to be . . . *enlightening.*

Like, I'd thought at first that Emma and Sam were simply going to be figureheads when it came to the building of the palace. That they'd shoot a few scenes showing them in charge, when in reality someone else would be making all of the decisions and overseeing whether things were getting done.

But they were both incredibly hands-on.

Sam had a clear vision for the layout of the structure. He knew he wanted three levels with multiple bedrooms, a jacuzzi big enough for both dogs out back, and a living room with a flat screen that would play different animal movies all day long. I learned through one of his confessionals that he'd been a few credits shy of having a degree in architecture before he dropped out of Columbia.

Emma was no slouch either.

She'd hired the same interior designer who had decorated their own mansion and was working side by side with her to outfit the pet palace when it was finished being built. For hours, the two pored over different hardwood floor swatches, doggy beds, furniture, and accent pieces. Everything from the shade of the light bulbs to the color, shape, and material of the dog dishes was decided on by the heiress herself.

It was actually quite impressive—if you could forget that they were doing all of this for a couple of dogs.

One day, while the crew was busy re-lighting a room, I took the opportunity to try to suss out where the zoo might be. Because so far, our search for the exotics had been a bust. And if we could just narrow it down, it'd make everything so much easier.

"Considering how big the palace is going to be, does that mean you see yourselves taking in more pets? Maybe a few rescues?" I asked while Emma sat in a chair with Lady Godiva on her lap. "Wait, are Lady Godiva and Titan the only animals you have right now?"

I asked this like it had only just dawned on me that there might be other furry friends on the property.

A sly smile spread across Emma's face. "There might be a few more critters running around," she said. "But *these* are our babies."

"And I can see why," I lied. "They *are* precious."

I leaned forward to pet the dog on Emma's lap, and she snapped at my hand and then growled.

"Sorry," Emma said, though she didn't actually sound all that apologetic. "Lady Godiva takes some time to warm up to people."

"*Ce n'est pas un problème,*" I said, waving her off.

It's no problem.

"I have found that many in your social circle have pets that are more . . . how you say . . . *sauvage?*" I said, pushing a little further.

Wild.

I knew it was a risk to pry, but I'd gotten closer to them over the past few days. They'd opened up about their upbringings, what it was like to live in the shadow of their grandfather, those crazy nights running around New York City with other rich kids. With everything they'd already divulged, I figured they might be willing to confide about their illegal dealings. Or at least give me something that would lead me to where they were hiding the exotics.

Emma's eyes flickered over to her brother, but he was simply staring off into the distance.

"Do they?" Emma answered cautiously. "I didn't know that. Then again, people don't exactly offer up their more . . . *questionable* life choices, do they? At least, around here they don't. Though, nothing surprises me anymore."

"So, there aren't any lion cubs running around?" I asked jokingly, in case I was going too far.

Silence.

Just when it was about to get uncomfortable, Sam suddenly let out a loud, barking laugh.

"Can you imagine?" he asked, laughing hysterically. Then, he stopped abruptly and put his finger up to his chin. "Though, I bet that might draw in the ladies. Chicks dig a guy that's a little dangerous, am I right? Hey, Em, maybe we *should* look into getting a lion."

Emma chuckled, too.

"Sorry, Brigeet, no lions here," she said to me, stroking Lady Godiva. "As much as we love animals—and we *totally* do—we're not really . . . *cat people.*"

I tried not to let my disappointment show.

They were good.

And I still didn't have any idea where the exotics were.

"Be careful not to say that in front of the film crew," I said conspiratorially. I pointed to the tiny microphone attached to the inside of her dress. "And always make sure your mic isn't on."

Emma's eyes grew wide and her hands flew to her neckline. When she was sure it had been turned off, she let out a breath.

"Way to look out," Sam said, nodding at me appreciatively.

"*Ce n'est rien,*" I said.

It's nothing.

A regal-looking man came in then and set down a tray of food for Emma and Sam.

"Do you guys want anything?" Emma asked as she grabbed a pear from the roundup.

"No, thank you," I said, waving her off. "We will leave you be so you can eat."

"All right," Sam said, already digging into some sushi that looked homemade—and delicious. "See you guys later."

Ollie and I scrambled to leave as quickly as we could

without literally running away. We hadn't had time that morning to search, and we still had so much ground to cover.

"Can I drive this time?" Ollie asked as we walked up to the cart.

"I don't know," I said hesitantly.

"Come on, Frankie!" he whined. "I haven't gotten to do *anything* fun yet. I did all that training after the last job so that I could play a bigger part this time. And all I've done so far is carry your bags and be ignored by the wonder twins back there."

"Your cover is as my assistant this time," I argued. "It's not like I'm *choosing* not to let you do anything. You're *doing* what an assistant does. And you're doing a great job!"

Ollie looked at me like he wanted to strangle me.

I gave him a smile and tried to look innocent.

But it didn't work. He knew my tricks too well by now.

I sighed.

"Okay," I conceded. "You can drive."

I handed him the keys and got in the passenger side.

"Really?" he asked, closing his hands over the keys like they were precious jewels about to be stolen. "I had this whole argument ready if you said no—"

"Would you rather me say no?" I asked him impatiently.

Ollie shook his head and jumped into the driver's seat.

"Where to?" he asked me, like he was now my personal driver.

170

I looked at the expanse of land in front of us.

"Driver's choice," I said, sinking into my seat and getting comfortable. Maybe having Ollie drive us from now on *would* be the smarter option. It's what an assistant would do, anyway.

I closed my eyes, soaking in the sun while simultaneously shivering in the cold as we crossed the uneven terrain.

My mind began to drift almost immediately.

What if we never found the exotics?

How long could we actually keep all this up before we were forced to head back to our regular lives?

We'd already called out sick from The Farm a few times, and the last thing I wanted to do was leave Kayla in a lurch.

Was it possible the animals weren't even on the twins' property? Maybe Emma and Sam had a special holding place for them somewhere else, that way their illegal dealings weren't directly tied to them.

"Frankie," Ollie said, interrupting my thoughts.

"Yeah," I said.

What if we never got the twins to admit to the trafficking and never found the animals? What if all of this was a waste of time?

"Uh, Frankie?" Ollie said again, more insistent this time.

I felt the cart begin to slow but didn't want to open my eyes just yet. If I didn't open them then none of what I'd just thought up could be true.

"What's up?" I asked Ollie reluctantly.

Before he could answer, a booming roar filled the air.

My eyes shot open then and I immediately took in the tiger that was pacing back and forth in front of us. I wasn't exactly an expert at reading cats, but it was pretty clear that the animal was agitated and on the hunt.

The question was, were we the prey?

Before I could think of how to escape, a scream caught in my throat as the tiger lunged right at us.

Entry Twenty-Four

The gigantic beast hit the side of the cage hard.

The metal container trembled, and for a hot second, I thought it might come down. Luckily, it stayed put.

But the tiger didn't.

He got back up like nothing had happened and began to pace his cage again.

My heart was pounding like it might pop out of my chest and I scrambled out of the passenger seat only to fall to the ground in shock. Though my legs felt like Jell-O, I managed to scoot backward across the dirt until my back hit something solid.

I was finding it hard to breathe with the adrenaline that was coursing through me, and knew that I needed to calm down, otherwise I could pass out.

Breathe in, two, three, four.

Breathe out two, three, four.

I fought to gain control over my body again, employing a calming technique Dad had taught me long ago. But the effects were short-lived.

Just as I felt myself begin to calm down, and let the reality wash over me that we had found the exotics, something brushed against my hair.

No.

Something *grabbed* my hair from behind.

I gazed upward and barely had a second to register what I was seeing before I lurched forward again.

A sharp pain exploded in my head as my wig was ripped away from my scalp—pins and all.

"Fffff-raaaccckkk!" I screamed before I could stop myself.

Crawling away on all fours, I came to a stop at the cart again, and turned back in disbelief. There, inside a cage, was an animal that looked like a really long-haired monkey—and it had my wig clutched in its claws!

"Holy guacamole!" Ollie exclaimed, still frozen in his spot behind the wheel. "Frankie, your hair!"

I reached up to touch my head, stopping at a spot I was sure was now bald. When I pulled my hand away, there was blood on it.

"I know," I groaned, as I discovered that the blood was actually from a gash I'd gotten on my palm while stumbling across the ground. "That stupid monkey has it."

"It's a sloth," Ollie corrected shakily.

"What?" I asked, feeling confused.

Wasn't confusion one of the signs of a concussion?

"It's not a monkey, it's a sloth," Ollie offered, his voice shaky.

"Well, whatever it is, it tried to scalp me," I said grumpily.

"Sloths are actually pretty docile," Ollie argued. "It most likely just saw your hair and grabbed for it out of curiosity. And then you freaked out and jerked away. . . ."

"So, it's *my* fault I have no hair?" I asked growing impatient.

I turned to look at Ollie for the first time since I'd jumped out of the car and saw that his face was completely white and his eyes were bugging out. He might very well have been in shock and I hadn't even noticed it.

"I'm sorry, Ollie," I forced out. "I'm not exactly thinking straight right now. Are you okay?"

His eyes met mine and seemed to finally focus, before giving me a tiny smile.

"I think so," he said, touching his chest and arms and face to make sure they were still there. "I *am* here, right? The tiger didn't eat us?"

"No," I said, standing up slowly. "But if it had, we would've gone down together, so at least there's that."

"Oh," Ollie said, still out of it. "That's good."

I tried to brush the dirt and dust off my jacket, but I knew it was a lost cause. The beautiful princess-style coat that I'd stolen and then kept in pristine condition for over four years was destroyed. I grabbed a piece of the pocket that had come apart at the seams and then dropped it again, feeling the pain of the moment as if it were physical.

As my focus shifted away from my messed-up frock,

I noticed for the first time that there were more than just those two cages in the area. There were at least a dozen more tiny enclosures surrounding us. I counted several other tigers, a few monkeys, a snake the size of an NBA player, a black panther, and a bear.

And then, of course, there was the sloth.

I turned and scowled at my nemesis, who was still holding on to my wig through the holes in its cage. Clenching my fists, I stomped over to it and grabbed the ball of hair out of its hands, and then attempted to brush out the knots with my fingers.

Grumbling under my breath, I took a second to glance at the sloth, who was still hanging along the edge of its cage. It had these enormous claws at the ends of its arms and legs that looked like pirate's hooks. Only, it was cuter than a pirate.

Way cuter, actually.

I tried to fight it—because I was still angry about my wig—but I couldn't help but break out into a smile.

The sloth cocked its black and white head to the side and stared back, the fur around its mouth making it appear like it had a perma-grin.

I pulled the wig over my head and pinned it back in place. My head still hurt, but the pain was starting to subside.

"No more grabbing my hair," I scolded the sloth good naturedly. "You have plenty of your own."

I was less than a foot away from it now, and began to

reach out my hand to pet it. Then I paused as I remembered Michaela's warning that wild animals never truly lost their instincts.

"Ollie, you said sloths are nice?" I asked him. "Like, it's not going to rip my arm off and beat me with it, right?"

"Shouldn't," Ollie said absently. "Three-toed sloths are the slowest moving mammals on the planet. My guess is its pretty chill."

I decided to take the chance and held my hand out to the creature, like you would to a dog. I had no idea if it wanted to be approached this way, but it was all I had.

And then I waited.

And waited.

Because Ollie was right. The sloth was soooo slow.

So slow, it seemed like the tiger even got bored.

From behind me, the big cat growled loudly. I turned just in time to see Ollie's whole body stiffen up again.

"That cage can hold him, right?" Ollie asked me, his voice trembling a bit.

I glanced at the enclosure with serious doubt.

"I really, really hope so," I said nervously.

"It'll hold—*for now*, at least," another voice said from out of nowhere. "But that could always change if the situation called for it."

Our heads snapped over to a walkway between the cages as a dark figure walked out and made its way toward us.

As the person got closer, it became clear it was a man—the scraggly beard gave that away—and he walked with a heavy limp on one side. He was wearing a long, dark blue jacket with a blue and white scarf coiling around his neck tightly like a noose. On top of his head sat a blue newsboy-style cap. A cigarette burned red between his lips, as he inhaled the smoke with every step, not even bothering to hold it with his fingers. One eye squinted at us, while the other remained wide open.

It took everything in me not to run away.

"And where did you two come from?" he asked us, his voice scratchy and gruff. The man slowly hobbled toward us, clutching onto something dark that swung back and forth with each step.

Then I watched with horror as something dripped from his hand and landed on the ground below. Just behind him, I could see that he'd left a trail of drops along the way.

I swallowed hard, my heart thumping.

"Eh, we are . . . guests of Mademoiselle Emma and Monsieur Sam," I said, forcing the French accent to come out despite my fear of the crazy man in front of us.

As he continued to close the distance between us, I forced myself to stand my ground and not retreat. Doing so would show him I was afraid and that he had the upper hand. I was also convinced it would reveal my age somehow. An adult wouldn't be scared of this old dude.

Well, actually, maybe they would.

"You with that TV crew?" he asked curiously.

And then, as if my vision had finally snapped into focus, I could see clearly what he was holding—and fought the urge to puke my guts out.

It was a rabbit.

A very dead rabbit.

I took a step back toward Ollie involuntarily, then kicked myself for flinching first.

The man raised a scraggly eyebrow as he followed my gaze down to the ball of fur in his hand.

"Oh," he grumbled, almost like he was noticing the bleeding animal for the first time. Then he held the messy carcass up in front of his body and gave us a grotesque smile. "It's lunchtime."

Ollie made a squeaking sound behind me and suddenly I could hear him breathing. Hard. Like he'd been running for miles. I was pretty sure he was close to hyperventilating.

Not that I blamed him. I felt like I might be headed that way myself.

The old man turned away from us then, staggering over to the tiger's cage, and throwing the rabbit up and over the top of the tall fence with zero fanfare.

As it soared through the air, flecks of blood caught on the wind and sprinkled the ground in front of us with tiny dots of red.

I heard Ollie gag. "I'm gonna throw up," he warned, before leaning over the side of the cart and retching.

The old man and I turned our focus to Ollie, but the tiger's eyes never left its meal. It tracked the flesh as it flew through the air and then leaped to catch it in its strong jaws before it could even touch the ground.

Then it swallowed it whole.

"I have eight more I have to feed," the old man barked. "Want to help?"

I opened my mouth, but nothing came out.

"You should wrap that up first, though," he continued, motioning with his head to the gash on my hand. "The cats'll go for fresh human blood before they'll go after the dead. It's like catnip to 'em. Get it? *Cat*nip?"

Then he let out a bellow of a laugh, making Ollie and I both flinch at the sound.

"Er, thanks for the offer," I said, practically falling into the cart's seat. "But we should probably get back."

I nudged Ollie to start the cart but he seemed frozen in place.

"Whatcher names?" the old guy asked us with a growl.

Crap.

This old creepy guy was going to sell us out.

"I am Brigeet and this is André," I said with my French-American accent. "And you are?"

"You can call me Cap'n Bob," he said.

Of course that was his name, because why not?

I got out of the cart again, even as my legs threatened to give out, and circled around to the other side.

Practically pushing Ollie into the passenger seat, I got in behind the wheel, not entirely sure I was in any better shape to drive as he was.

"Well, okay," I said, wanting nothing more than to get out of there. "Nice to meet you."

Cap'n Bob stared at us, his one eye squinting menacingly.

"Maybe I'll see you around," he said. "We don't get a lot of visitors back here. At least, none that stick around long."

And with that, I started the engine and gunned it.

Entry Twenty-Five

This will be my last journal entry.

Ever.

Because I'm done.

I'm done being a thief.

I'm done thinking I'm in control of every situation when clearly, I'm not.

I'm done because I'm not as good as I thought.

I'm done because I could've gotten Ollie killed with all this animal business.

I'm done.

I'm done.

I'm.

Done.

Entry One

She's not done.

She's just freaking out.

Oh, this is Ollie, btw.

And I found this journal in the trash.

I didn't even know Frankie wrote in a journal, but here it is.

It took every ounce of willpower I had not to read what's in these pages, but I respect Frankie's privacy.

Okay, I read her last entry, but I wasn't entirely sure what this notebook was until I'd already started reading it. But I swear I stopped after that.

If you're reading this, Frankie, please don't kill me.

All right, back to the facts.

Like I said before, Frankie freaked out after the whole "zoo" debacle and ended up barricading herself in her room for days on end.

Yes, that's an exaggeration, but when they make this into a movie, it will be far more exciting than what she actually did.

Which was to retreat to her room, get into bed, pull the covers up over her head and block out the world for a good thirty-one hours. I don't know what she thought about during that time. I don't know if she binge-watched any shows. I don't know anything except that I didn't hear from her, and then when I called the house, the Detective told me she hadn't come out of her room in over a day.

So, I hightailed over here to snap her out of it.

When I finally broke down her door (again, I've exaggerated for entertainment purposes), I found her still curled up in a ball. She might've even been crying! I'm not actually sure about this though, because I was distracted by how bad it smelled in her room.

It was like she hadn't changed her clothes since she'd rolled around in the dirt at the zoo.

Turned out, I was right.

So, I ordered her to take a shower.

She obliged because I can be very persuasive when I want to be.

She also might have caught a whiff of herself and nearly passed out from the smell.

I'd like to take this opportunity to say a few—

Entry Twenty-Six

Sorry about that.

Had to teach Ollie a little something called "boundaries."

Now, where was I?

Oh, yeah . . . Ollie was right about a few things (though I'll never admit it to him).

I'm not done.

I was just having a . . . moment back there.

But now I'm back.

The second thing he was right about was, I *did* sort of go into hiding for a day or two after the incident at the zoo. During that time, I slept and did *not* cry, and attempted to block out the feelings of guilt I was having over what I'd done.

I also may have watched an episode or two of *Game of Thrones*.

But even that didn't help.

Because the truth was, I hadn't done my job to keep Ollie and I safe. I'd jumped the gun and put our lives in jeopardy. And for what? To prove to Dad that I could make my own decisions?

Clearly, I couldn't make good ones.

And at the time, I wasn't even sure if Ollie was talking to me anymore. We were both so thrown by our experience with the exotics that we hadn't talked on our way back to the main house.

And then we didn't talk some more on our way home.

And then we continued to not talk the following day.

It was just radio silence.

So, I assumed he didn't want to have anything to do with me.

And I didn't blame him. This whole heist had been a failure of epic proportions so far. Then there was the zoo, and all the ways we could have been hurt—well, that was just the icing on a moldy old cake of suckage.

I was usually far more prepared on a job. It was something Dad had always been really good at. Anticipating all the things that could go wrong and planning for them, so it didn't throw us off our goal.

I definitely hadn't been prepared for just how dangerous this job would be. And I wasn't even sure what our goal was anymore.

Originally, it had been to simply rob the twins for the horrible crimes they'd been committing—trafficking the exotics and leading to their mistreatment and deaths—and then turn them in to the cops and spread the money we'd gotten from the job, around to animal rights organizations, sanctuaries, and rescues.

But as I'd learned more about the world of exotic

animal trading, it became clear that most traders, even when caught, were given little to no consequences for their actions. Sure, it would've hurt them to lose some of their money, but it wouldn't truly be justice if the actual trafficking didn't stop.

And I wanted the consequences.

Especially after seeing how these animals were being treated. Kept in cages barely bigger than their own bodies, malnourished despite the money that the twins were putting into their "pet palace," and who knew what Cap'n Bob was doing to them when no one was looking?

The other downside to letting the cops handle things? Their way often meant killing the animals instead of tranquilizing them and delivering them to rescues. The idea of these animals being tortured for most of their lives only to be euthanized when help finally came made me sad.

And angry.

So, leaving the animals on the property and simply taking the cash didn't seem like a viable option anymore. In the end, I wanted everyone to be safe *and* the twins behind bars.

But how was I supposed to make that happen without putting lives in jeopardy? Because as skilled as I may be at stealing things, even I knew I was in over my head on this one.

And if I tried to handle the tigers myself I might just lose my own life.

That's as far as I'd gotten when Ollie burst through my door (he did *not* break it down) and started complaining about the smell, which I'd like to say for the record, was not as bad as he made it out to be.

All those hours of feeling guilty and sorry for myself, and I still didn't have a plan.

I knew how to steal money, diamonds, art—but I had no idea how to steal a small zoo of dangerous, exotic animals.

Luckily, my partner did.

Entry Twenty-Seven

It felt like we were heading right back into the lion's den.

"We have to be prepared for the possibility that the twins already know that we were snooping around," I reminded Ollie as we drove our golf cart up the long driveway to their house. "So, if they confront us, let me do the talking, okay?"

"Not a problem," Ollie said, holding his hair in place so it didn't blow away in the wind. "Besides, I've got my own stuff to take care of today."

He looked over at me and beamed.

I'd finally had to admit that maybe we weren't utilizing all of Ollie's unique skills and talents when it came to pulling off this heist. It wasn't that I didn't think he was capable of a bigger role. I think it was just hard for me to relinquish control. But at some point you have to hope you've taught your protégé well enough that they can stand on their own.

Like Dad had done with me.

It was time to let Ollie fly solo.

At least a little bit.

"Yes, you do," I said, trying not to make a big deal

out of it. I didn't want to psych him out. "Just stick to the plan and you'll be fine."

"Right," Ollie said, still smiling like a goofball.

"And Ollie?"

"Yeah?" he asked.

"French men don't smile that much," I said.

Ollie's face fell into a frown.

"Right," he said.

"Better," I answered. "Remember, *ABC*."

"One, two, three?" Ollie guessed slowly, scrunching up his face.

"No," I said, rolling my eyes. "Always Be in Character."

"Right," he said, nodding his head. Then in his horrible French-American accent, he added, "I am André, a boring, annoyed French man. I am Brigeet's assistant and pretty much hate my life."

"Hey!" I exclaimed. "I treat my assistants well!"

Ollie shrugged unaffected. "Eh."

"Watch out or I'll fire you," I teased as we arrived at the main house and I parked the cart.

We walked up to the front door and went inside without knocking. Ever since the twins had begun filming, they'd instituted an open-door policy. As in, they weren't going to come and open the door for anyone. Not with that many people milling around at least.

People were expected to just let themselves in.

So, we did.

Once inside, we went up to the first crew member

we saw and asked where they were filming for the day. The girl, who was sitting in the middle of the living room untangling cables, pointed us in the direction of the backyard and then went back to her task.

Lights were set up in nearly every corner of the house, making it feel much more like we were on a very elaborate set than in somebody's house. People sat around tapping away on their phones or talking into their walkies to other crew members posted around the property.

"Perfect timing," I muttered to Ollie as we walked back outside and into the chilly air. "They must be on a break from filming."

"Or they haven't started yet," Ollie offered. "You know how long it takes them to get glammed up."

"Good point," I said. "Well, let's see what we're working with today."

We walked up to the twins, who were lounging in folding chairs that had their names across the backs. Emma was wrapped in what looked like a furry, wearable blanket, her cheeks rosy and eyes focused on her phone in her gloved hands. Sam sat in the other chair, his legs crossed, trying to find an angle he liked with his phone's camera.

"This light is washing me out," Sam complained, dropping his arms into his lap. "I look like I should be in the hospital."

"California has the best hospitals," Emma said dreamily. "Remember the suite they put Mom in at that hospital in LA? It was better than the Four Seasons."

"Sick people bum me out," Sam muttered, holding his phone back up to his face and moving his head around to find an angle that worked.

Finally, he sighed loudly and looked around until he found a crew member working nearby. "You! Yeah, you. Hey, man, can you call your buddies and tell them to get makeup out here? I need them to fix this whole situation."

Sam twirled his finger around his face, not bothering to wait for a reply from the guy, before collapsing back into his seat.

"I think you both look *ravishing*," I said in Brigeet's accent, walking up to them and taking hold of Emma's hands earnestly before leaning in and giving her a kiss on both cheeks. I did the same with Sam before taking a step back.

"I didn't know you were coming today," Emma said. She didn't sound unhappy, exactly. Maybe a little surprised. "I was beginning to wonder if you'd ever come back."

"Ah, yes. So sorry," I answered. "It turns out running a magazine from outside the country is not so easy a feat."

"I can only imagine," Emma said, looking more closely at me now.

My instincts were to shrivel up under her scrutiny, but it's not what Brigeet would do, so I stood a little taller instead. I was wearing a full-length turtleneck sweater dress today. The sleeves of which extended past my wrists and over my hands with chic thumbholes. And while it was no doubt fashionable, the reason I'd chosen it was because it covered up the wound on my hand, as well as all the other little scratches and scrapes I'd gotten while visiting the exotics.

I'd topped it off with some knee-high boots and my signature sunglasses and knew that no one would be able to see past the disguise.

"That outfit is *life*," Emma purred. "But ten minutes with it on and I'd be *covered* in dog fur."

She pulled open her blanket coat and Lady Godiva popped her head out. As soon as she saw me, she began to growl.

"Now, now," Emma said softly, petting the spot between the dog's eyes. Within seconds, she'd calmed down and fallen asleep.

"So, do we need to talk about the drama?" Emma asked me after a few seconds.

Here we go. She was about to bust us for sneaking around. I braced myself for the confrontation.

"Drama?" I asked, coolly. "I don't know what you are talking about."

Emma's eyes flitted over to Sam briefly, but he didn't seem to be listening to us at all.

"Oh, I was sure that you'd heard," Emma said languidly. "Turns out there's another doghouse being made that's bigger than our original plans. So, we did some creative problem solving and . . . we're adding another story!"

"*Sensationnel*," I exclaimed, though I wanted to roll my eyes.

How many rescue animals could've been saved with the money they were spending on another story of a dog-house for two dogs?

The whole thing was absolutely ridiculous.

"What great news!" I said, matching Emma's smile. "André, why don't you go on over to the construction site and find out what changes have been made to the original plans."

"Hey, I'll head over there with you, man," Sam said, surprising all of us.

It hadn't seemed like he'd been listening, but apparently he had. I'd have to remember that in the future. Say the wrong thing around him and it could screw things up royally.

"Uh, *oui*," Ollie said, his eyes widening at me.

"There's this construction chick over there that I've been trying to talk to," Sam said, straightening his sweater and running his hand through his hair.

Ollie pursed his lips at me, before following in Sam's footsteps down to where the crew was busy putting up one of the walls of the structure.

"Well then," Emma said, turning back to me. "Should we get going then?"

"Going?" I asked, confused.

Emma gathered the blankets around her body and stood up, dog and all.

"I thought we'd start that interview for the magazine now . . . ," she said. "No better time than the present, right?"

I looked over at where Ollie was standing, his back to me and already engaging in a conversation with a few of the workers. He was busy with his part of the plan and I needed to get on with mine.

I nodded in agreement.

"Very true," I said, and got up to follow her. "Where shall we do this then?"

Emma looked back over her shoulder at me as she climbed the steps to the house.

"Oh, I've got a place in mind," she said slyly, and then disappeared inside.

Entry Twenty-Eight

"And this is my mindfulness studio," Emma said, pushing open a door on our right with considerable fanfare.

I poked my head inside the space and nodded.

It was a nearly empty room, not unlike a typical workout space or dance studio. One of the walls was all mirrors and there were shelves in the corner with towels, exercise mats, and bottles of water. In another section of the room, there was just a pile of pillows and mats. A tiny table in the center held a variety of aromatherapy bottles, a diffuser, essential oils, and lotions.

"I like to come in here when I want to escape and just basically get centered," Emma said calmly. Before closing the door again, she bowed to the empty room. "*Namaste.*"

Okay.

We left the room and continued down the hallway.

"And down here we have something really special," she said, suddenly jumping up and down like a little kid.

"I can hardly wait," I said, forcing enthusiasm into my voice.

Emma had taken the last fifteen minutes to give me the grand tour of her side of the house. And while it was indeed, impressive—there was a theater, a nightclub, and a full spa setup, complete with a mudroom—it was also a huge time suck.

We came to a door at the end of the hallway and Emma took a key from around her neck and stuck it in the lock.

Well, what's this, then? A secret locked door? Now we're talking.

"Are you ready?" she asked, creating a buildup I really hoped paid off in the end.

Before turning the key, the heiress brought her hand up to the keypad near the frame and typed in six numbers. When the light on the pad turned from red to blue, she turned the key in the lock and then pushed the heavy door open.

"Should I be worried?" I joked around as I looked inside. It was pitch black. I could only see as far as the light in the hallway would shine.

"Not if you're with me," she said, smiling.

Emma reached out into the dark and suddenly lights sprang on, one by one, all the way down the length of the room. Suddenly I could see that it was just another white hallway. There were no pictures, no pieces of art. Nothing. Just white everywhere.

I started to take a step forward, but Emma stopped me.

"Not yet," she warned, placing her palm firmly on my shoulder. Then she handed me a pair of ugly sunglasses.

"It's no worry. I've got my own," I said, raising and lowering my sunglasses over my eyes.

"Just put them on," she said, sounding bored.

I turned my head and did as I was told, only to be rewarded with something I never imagined.

Under the lens of the glasses, I could see glowing red lasers. Dozens of them. Low to the ground, as high as my head. They went diagonal, straight across and a few even split the middle of the room.

They were everywhere, and I would've walked right into them if Emma hadn't warned me.

I looked over at her and she looked absolutely giddy. Like a kid on Christmas morning.

I could tell she wanted me to be impressed.

And I was.

But I was also excited. Because, of course, lasers had to mean there was something important on the other side of the hallway. You don't install an alarm system like that for no reason.

"Are you hiding something crazy in there?" I teased. "Because if you are, our readers want to know."

"Hiding something, yes. Crazy . . . well, it's all relative, right?" Emma asked, waving her hand in the air.

She pulled out her phone, and after moving her thumbs around in rapid motion, I watched the lasers disappear.

The alarm was controlled from her cell.

"Cool, huh?" she asked me before leading the way down the hallway and toward the room ahead.

I followed willingly, curious what was inside.

If I'd known, I might not have followed.

"Oh, I've been meaning to ask you something, Bri-geet," Emma said casually, stopping just inside.

That was when I heard the growl.

And then I let out a shriek as something punctured my leg.

Looking down in horror, I saw that there was a tiny tiger trying to use my leg as a chew toy. As a reflex, I shook my leg like it was on fire and the little ball of fur let go and scampered across the room to its other buddies.

I turned my head in shock to stare at Emma, who was standing there, one hand on her hip, the other holding Lady Godiva.

"How's your hand doing after visiting our little pet-ting zoo the other day?" she asked, her face blank. "Did you find what you were looking for?"

Entry Twenty-Nine

I was so shaken by the turn of events that I couldn't decide who was more dangerous right now: the tigers or Emma.

My mouth had gone dry and I had to swallow hard before attempting to answer her.

"I *knew* you were a lover of exotic animals too!" I exclaimed finally, thinking fast.

Emma blinked at me. She obviously hadn't expected me to say this.

"Too?" she asked skeptically.

"*Oui*," I said, forcing myself to walk across the room, bypassing small cages along the way.

There was a long rip in my sweater dress from where the baby had latched on, but I think I'd managed to get away without it clawing a hole through my skin. Which was good, because I didn't want to find out what they would do if they smelled blood.

"As soon as Mr. Miles told me that you'd supplied him with his beloved tiger, I knew that I'd found a kindred spirit."

My head was screaming for me to run away, but I needed to keep my cover, so I forced myself to bend down and pet the baby tiger.

"Christian told you that he got his tiger from us?" Emma asked, sounding a little peeved. "That . . . blabbermouth. He's usually better at keeping secrets than that. I guess Karma gets you in the end, after all."

And what will Karma have in store for you?

"That whole situation with the police was an absolute tragedy," I said, shaking my head. "I can only hope your other clients don't suffer the same fate."

Emma went to the door and placed Lady Godiva on the floor, the dog running on her tippy toes back down the hallway to safety.

I wanted to do the same.

"We'll be making sure our other clients are more careful in the future," Emma added.

"A smart decision," I said, nodding. "One bad apple could bring down the whole tree. A tree that I'm keenly interested in hearing about. Possibly being a part of . . ."

I let my words trail off. It had dawned on me over the past couple of days that the only way I'd be able to take down their whole operation was if I were a part of it.

Or at least I needed them to think I was a part of it.

Emma raised her eyebrow at me, as she took in what I was implying.

I decided she needed a tiny nudge in the right direction.

"I mean, if you would like to continue your venture on your own, best wishes," I said, turning my back like I didn't care either way. "But if you want to take things to the next level, I believe I could help you . . . go international."

"Sam and I *have* been talking about how to step things up," Emma said, chewing on her lip thoughtfully. "Grandfather is always saying that we think too small. And it's true that Huntington Diamonds only hit a billion when they expanded."

I just nodded as I moved around the room. I could tell that I didn't need to do anything else to convince her. She was going to convince herself.

"So, this is where you keep the babies, then?" I asked her as I ran my hand across one of the cages.

"Huh?" Emma asked, lost in her thoughts.

"You obviously keep the others out on your property with that zookeeper of yours," I said, making a face.

"Um, yeah," Emma said. When she saw my face, she sighed. "I know, he's sort of . . . rough around the edges, but Cap'n Bob is good with the animals and is loyal."

"Is that how you knew we'd discovered your hidden zoo?"

Emma nodded.

"But I don't think he meant to rat you out or anything," she said. "Bob just mentioned that a couple who spoke a different language had shown up. You were the only ones I could think of."

"And you brought me here to see if I was a friend or foe?" I suggested.

"Something like that," Emma said, a smile growing across her face.

"And how did I do?" I asked, as if I already knew the answer.

"I'll let you know once I figure it out," she said carefully.

"Fair enough," I answered. "Tell me about all of this." I motioned to the room around us.

I thought she might protest, but her face seemed to light up as I asked.

"This is the Jungle Room," she said proudly. "All the plants are native to the animals' original homes, and the temperature is set to create the perfect environment for them."

"Animals?" I asked, having only seen the tigers. "What else do you have hidden around this palatial estate?"

"Oh, you're going to love this!" Emma said and practically skipped over to the opposite side of the room. With all the fanfare she could muster, she pulled back some oversized greenery, revealing a ginormous glass encasement.

"Well, what do we have here?" I continued in my French-American accent.

I took a few steps closer and stuck my face up against the glass. And then I searched. Out of the corner of my eye, I saw something move.

No.

I saw something slither.

And then suddenly it was flying toward my head from the other side of the glass and I was jolting backward.

What was with these animals attacking me!

I looked at the terrarium from a distance now and saw the giant snake's head moving back and forth slowly as its beady eyes followed me.

"What a . . . magnificent creature," I said, trying not to show how utterly creeped out I was. "It is a . . ."

"It's a yellow anaconda," Emma supplied. "Isn't she just the cutest!"

Emma stepped toward the glass and tickled it with her fingers as if the snake could feel it. I'm not sure if it was because the snake recognized her or it had smelled my fear, but the giant reptile didn't seem to have the same visceral reaction to her than she had me.

"I can see why you call it the Jungle Room," I said, laughing nervously.

"This was an idea I had a few years back," Emma said, going over to an oversized ottoman and laying down. There were scratches all over it. Rips in the velvet, where stuffing was peeking out. The idea that the same could be done to my skin didn't make me any more comfortable to be in there. "I used to only bring the baby tigers out for parties, but then I figured why not let them live in here? I mean, until they get too big and I have to sell them, of course."

"How old are these guys?" I asked, watching a few of

them roll around on the floor together. Then, my heart started to hammer as one of them jumped up onto the ottoman next to Emma and started to paw at her hair.

"Penelope!" Emma said, sitting up and pulling the cat to her. Even as a baby, it barely fit in her lap, and the way it was wriggling around, I was worried she was going to lose a finger.

Or an eye.

"Not the hair!" she said giggling. Then she turned to me again. "Penelope here is the oldest. She's about five months old."

I flinched in surprise.

I'm pretty sure Michaela had said that tigers started to get dangerous to handle around three months? And this one was nearly twice that.

As I wrapped my head around this, Penelope let out a little growl, until Emma turned her over and tickled her belly. The cat began to mouth Emma's hands until she pulled her hand away abruptly.

"Gentle!" Emma scolded. She stood up from the ottoman and brought her wound up to her mouth. "Ow."

"Maybe it's time these kitties graduated to a bigger cage?" I suggested, slowly backing away from the two tigers who'd been wrestling earlier but now seemed interested in me.

"Eh, they're fine," Emma said, waving her hand in the air. "They'd never hurt their mommy."

"Okay," I said, silently disagreeing. "So, answer me

this: Why did you get into the whole exotic trade industry?"

"Off the record?" Emma asked, raising her eyebrow doubtfully.

"Of course," I said. "All of this is off the record. I don't want to get caught either, you know."

"Right," Emma answered. "Well, it started when Sam and I were heading over to Africa for a quick vacation, and one of my heiress friends asked us to bring her back a monkey. At first I thought she was crazy, but then I made a few calls and discovered it was supes easy to buy an exotic animal. There are no laws about it, and they charge next to nothing over there."

Correction, there are laws. They just don't always apply to rich people.

"When we delivered the hairy thing to my friend, she paid us a finder's fee of ten grand. And that got us thinking," Emma said, slinking back over to the snake tank. "Our grandfather was getting ready to update his will—something he does every four years, or whenever one of us messes up—and he'd been riding us about finding our own ways to contribute to the family fortune. So, we figured, sure, we'll sell animals to our friends. And it's proven to be very lucrative."

"But a little in the gray area as far as your government goes, no?" I asked. "I imagine you keep these business dealings—along with the profits you've made—how you say . . . to yourselves?"

I wanted to lead her into talking about the fortune they'd no doubt accrued since they'd begun trafficking animals for a living. Over the years of robbing the rich, I'd learned that wealthy people kept their clean money in banks. But their real money, the stuff made by shadier means, was kept somewhere the IRS couldn't get to it.

I wanted *that* money.

The dirty money. Because if given to the right people, I might just be made clean again.

Emma tapped the side of her nose, the universal symbol for being right about something.

"Yet another thing our family is good at—hiding money," Emma said, oddly proud.

"Well, color me intrigued," I said, feeding her ego. I could tell she wanted to brag about how clever she and her brother were. "Maybe I could learn something from you. I've just been using off-shore accounts to hide my more . . . indelicate dealings. Do you have a better idea?"

Emma looked like she was considering telling me everything.

But then a voice asked from the entrance to the room, "You think she can keep a secret?"

Both of us turned quickly to see Sam standing there, leaning up against the door frame.

I had no idea how long he'd been there.

Was this going to be a problem now?

"Still not sure. I mean, she wants to do business with us. Help us expand into the international market," Emma said, seeming to scrutinize me. Suddenly she threw her hands in the air and yelled out, "What the heck. I have a good feeling about you, Brigeet. And my gut's never wrong."

Until now.

"What about . . . insurance?" Sam reminded his sister.

"Right!" Emma smacked her head. "Duh. Okay, come on over here, *partner*."

Emma grabbed my hand—yes, the injured one—and pulled me across the room, calling for the cats to come. They obliged and soon there were five not-so-little tigers surrounding us. She picked up the smallest one and handed it to me.

The animal was so heavy, I nearly dropped it. Luckily, the cat dug its claws into my arms and stayed upright.

"What is happening?" I asked, managing to keep my accent going.

"We like to get a little . . . collateral just in case people think about getting chatty," she said, putting her arm around me. "Say cheese."

"Cheese," I said robotically, still not quite knowing why we were taking a picture.

"Got it," Sam said, nodding at the photo he'd taken of us on his phone.

"And we took the picture because . . . ," I started.

"Because we want you to know that if we go down, so do you," Sam explained. "And this picture's all the proof we need."

Too bad all they had was a picture of a fictional French magazine editor.

"Right," I said, not bothering to argue. "So, tell me all your secrets."

"Well, you have to do a lot more to earn all of them," Emma said. "But here's a little something for you."

Emma motioned for me to join her back over by the anaconda cage. I did not want to go. But I did anyway.

When I got there, she put her arm around my shoulder like we were going into a huddle.

"Grandfather taught us that the best place to hide your money is in a place nobody wants to go. I won't give away his hiding spot, but I'll let you in on ours," she said, pointing inside the cage and then turning on a little spotlight so we could see better.

"Holy diamonds!" I exclaimed before I could stop myself.

They were everywhere. Gems and jewels of all sizes, shapes, and colors. Just thrown around the cage amongst the snake poop. Emma was right. Nobody was going in there to steal their stuff anytime soon.

"I know!" Emma exclaimed. "Isn't it wild? It's like really expensive glitter!"

"Most of them are conflict diamonds, gifted to us by our grandfather so we obviously can't sell them. Well, in *stores* anyway," Sam explained. "And the larger ones, well, our girl likes those the best. She uses them as pillows."

My jaw had fallen open at some point, and I forced it closed before the twins realized how gobsmacked I was.

"There has to be millions of dollars in there," I breathed.

"And there's more," Emma said excitedly.

"Are you going to tell me the leaves are made out of hundred dollar bills next?"

"Ha!" Sam let out a loud guffaw and pointed at me. "You're funny."

I nodded kindly.

"So, the real treasure's . . ." I let my words drift off, hoping one of them would answer.

And after a brief pause, Emma did.

"Right there," she said, pointing to something in the back of the cage.

I squinted through the glass, trying not to be distracted by the giant snake and hundreds of diamonds littering the ground. It wasn't easy, but finally I saw it.

There, inside the snake enclosure and behind the two-hundred-pound anaconda, was a safe.

"All our *real* valuables are in there," she whispered in my ear, before leaving me gaping behind her as she walked away.

Entry Thirty

I've heard of guard dogs, but guard *snakes*?

This was definitely a first for me—and I'd been to a lot of secret hiding spots.

By the time we made our way back outside, I was itching to tell Ollie what the twins had just revealed. He might actually die. Like fall down dead. He wouldn't go near the boa constrictor when we were at The Farm, no way was he going to even begin to approach a twelve-foot-long anaconda.

Even for a million dollars.

There's a chance he wouldn't even go inside the house again, knowing it was there.

As soon as I walked out the door, I immediately scanned the area for him. But just as I did, Emma called me back.

"Oh, Brigeet!" she said all singsongy.

I sighed, my back to her, before plastering on a big smile and turning around.

"Oui?" I said.

Sam had come up behind Emma and threw his arms around his sister's neck, placing his head near hers. Was it a twin thing that made them that close?

It was always like they were attached at the hip. I didn't get it. Weren't siblings supposed to hate each other most of the time?

I wondered how they'd cope when they were separated by jail cells.

"We're having a dinner party on Saturday night," Emma said. "Some of our clients will be attending. Might be a good opportunity for you to meet everyone."

"That sounds splendid," I said. "Count me in."

Before I could turn around, Sam had closed the distance between us and leaned in close to me. "These are very important clients, Brigeet. One is Geo Ford, the eccentric billionaire, who has requested eight adult tigers and a few other animals, so that he can throw a hunting party on his property later this month."

"Wait, he's buying them just to *hunt* them?" I asked incredulously.

Sam nodded.

"One of the others is supermodel turned designer, Thoya Vanderhook," he continued.

"Please tell me she doesn't want to make them into furs?" I pleaded. I was joking at first but then I saw his face and felt mine fall.

"Hey, I try not to judge," Sam said, holding his hands up in the air defensively. "That's not going to be a problem for you, is it?"

Um, yeah.

"Not at all," I said, trying to seem cool about it. "I just like to know what I'm dealing with."

"Great! There are a few others, too, but we haven't finalized the guest list yet," he said, starting to walk back toward Emma. "This is gonna be a big night, Brigeet. Be sure to bring your A-game!"

Oh, I'll bring it.

I nodded and walked away as quickly as I could.

When I finally caught up with Ollie, he was still engaged in an intense conversation with a few of the TV crew guys.

I caught his eye when he was just about to say something to one of the guys wearing a headset and carrying a walkie. I gave him an imperceptible nod and began to walk in the direction of our cart.

Ollie clapped the guy on the back and said his good-byes before hurrying over to catch up with me.

"You were gone awhile," he said, a little bit winded from the run. "Everything okay?"

"Not even a little bit," I said, and then regaled him with stories of the Jungle Room, the baby tigers, the anaconda, and the money.

When I told him that the twins' fortune was hidden inside the snake tank, he practically turned white.

"Wait, why am I tripping?" he asked out loud a few seconds later. "It's not like *I'm* going into the cage. That's all you, girl. Good luck with that."

I rolled my eyes at him.

"Thanks for the vote of confidence," I said as we got into the golf cart.

"How are you gonna do it?" he asked, curiously.

I shook my head. "No clue," I said. "I'm prepared for the lasers, the keypad, a safe—that's normal thief stuff. But sneaking past a giant snake? That's new territory for me. I've gotta reach deep for this one. Feel free to make any suggestions, though."

Ollie rubbed his chin as if he were thinking.

"I'll give it some thought and get back to you," he answered.

"You do that."

I steered us in the direction of the secret zoo on the property. Now that everything was out in the open with the twins and their exotic dealings, we needed to get a closer look at exactly what we'd be stealing.

We had the plan, now we just had to work out the details.

I could feel my adrenaline start to rev back up as we got closer.

It seemed too soon to be going back into a situation with wild animals, but unfortunately, we didn't have the luxury of time.

We were going to be pulling this heist the night of the dinner party.

When I'd told Ollie that we would be putting our plan into motion in a few short days, he'd just nodded.

"*Of course* we are," he'd said, not bothering to fight me on it. "Because, why wait?"

By now, he was used to me giving him a short turn-around on things with no explanation. I think he'd actually even started to expect it.

But this time there was an actual reason for keeping things speedy: part of my plan was time sensitive. And it was integral to pulling everything off.

"Did you get all the info we needed from the construction crew?" I asked Ollie, talking just loudly enough to be heard over the wind in our ears from driving.

Ollie nodded while holding his wig down.

"The crew enters through the back of the property. There's a larger maintenance entrance just past the zoo," he explained. "That's how they bring in the equipment and building materials. There's only one guy working back there, and apparently he spends most of his time on his phone, so it should be an easy access point."

"Great," I said. Then I glanced sideways at him as I pulled into the cover of the trees. "Looked like you were getting pretty social back there. Making friends with the TV crew now, are we?"

"Don't worry, you're still my number one," Ollie joked. "But, yeah, those guys had a lot of . . . interesting things to say about the twins," Ollie disclosed.

"Like?"

"Like, they keep forgetting that they're mic'd and the

sound guys are getting some pretty nutso stuff behind the scenes," he said.

My eyes grew big.

"They haven't heard any of our conversations, have they?" I asked, suddenly worried. I may have been in disguise and taken on a pretty foolproof accent, but it was never a good idea to leave behind concrete evidence like that.

Ollie shook his head.

"So far, Emma curses like a sailor when she's alone and talks to Lady Godiva *all* the time. Full-on conversations with the dog," he said. "And Sam . . . well, let's just say he's already *made friends* with several girls on both crews. And none of them know about each other. They say his ability to woo is unreal."

I rolled my eyes.

"Geez," I muttered. "Okay, so I need to be more aware of their mics from here on out."

"Probably a good idea," Ollie agreed as the cages took shape in front of us.

This time I was ready for what we saw.

I parked the cart and took a deep breath before stepping down into the dirt.

"Let's try *not* to get mauled on this visit?" Ollie said. It should've been a joke, but it came out deadly serious.

"Agreed," I answered, walking over to the sloth's cage first.

Its eyes had turned our way as we drove up and they

hadn't moved since. Neither had his body. The little guy was like a furry statue being kept behind bars.

"Hey there, friend," I said, going over to the cage and placing my hand on one of the bars out of his reach. He was cute, but not so cute that I was going to risk losing my arm by sticking it in his cage to pet him.

The sloth uncurled its hand from the bar one excruciatingly slow finger at a time, until it was finally free and he slowly outstretched his arm to where I was standing.

"I know," I said, feeling like we were able to communicate despite not speaking the same language. "You're not gonna be stuck here forever, little guy. Just hang tight a little longer."

"You know you're talking to a sloth," Ollie called out, leaving the safety of our cart but not going too far.

"And?" I challenged.

"And nothing," he said with a shrug. "Just making sure you recognized that."

"Noted," I said and stood back up before turning to look at the tiger that would've eaten me the other day if given the chance. "And then there's *you*."

The big cat roared at me as if confirming my thoughts.

"Don't worry," I said to it. "We're breaking you out, too."

I stepped closer to the enclosure, while making sure to remain way out of the danger zone. I had to get a closer look at the cage.

I took out my camera and zoomed in, taking a few dozen pictures of the lock and hinges, and then stepped back again.

"There are no bars on the ground," I observed. "I'm shocked none of the animals have dug their ways out."

"A few have tried," a man's gruff voice interjected.

I heard the telltale shuffle before I saw him.

"You two again?" Cap'n Bob said, showing up again as if out of nowhere. "I thought I'd scared ye off last time."

How did he manage to sneak up on people when he was such a loud walker?

"We were hoping to get a proper tour this time," I said, like this was a normal request.

Cap'n Bob eyed us suspiciously, before walking slowly over to me, sliding his bad leg along behind him.

"Did ye now?" he asked, stopping just two feet away from me, fully invading my space.

He smelled like animal poop and something sour.

"We're going to be working with Emma and Sam on a few . . . projects," I continued, walking around Cap'n Bob and heading closer to the tiger cage. At that particular moment, the animal seemed less threatening than the man in front of us. "We were wondering if you could answer a few questions."

"I don't see how I have a choice, now do I?" Cap'n Bob said. My back was to him, but I could hear the sneer in his voice. "The masters told me that if you came back

218

around, I was to make myself available to you for whatever you needed."

"Wonderful," I said, acting like I didn't notice the disdain he was emulating. "So, how many tigers do you guys have on the property?"

"Come with me," was all he said in response.

I looked over at Ollie and shrugged. We both began to follow the creepy caretaker. I followed the line he was drawing in the dirt with his bum leg and stayed over an arm's-length away from any of the cages we passed.

"We currently have twelve tigers on the grounds. Eight arc adults. We have a shipment coming in next week that will add eleven more to that number," Cap'n Bob said. "Most of 'em will be shipped back out to buyers within the week, though some will be deemed not worthy and might stay here until we can find someone to take them or we'll *have to take care of them.*"

"They'll just live here for the rest of their lives?" I asked, feeling bad for the animals that would be stuck in tiny cages for their whole miserable existences.

"No," Cap'n Bob said, not bothering to sugarcoat anything. "I mean, they'll be euthanized if they can't be sold."

"They'll be killed?"

"What else are they gonna do with them?" Cap'n Bob asked me. "At least this way they can make some money selling the parts."

The animals were like stolen cars to them. It was disgusting.

"Oh," I said, being careful not to come off as excessively emotional over the animals since clearly, nobody else cared.

As we walked down the aisle, there were tigers on every side of us. They all varied in size, but even the smallest one was huge.

All of them seemed angry.

Were we really going to be able to pull this off?

"How do you clean the cages?" I asked Cap'n Bob.

As horrendous as their dwellings were, at least they weren't lying in their own filth. In fact, to his credit, it looked like the Cap'n did a pretty good job at taking care of them day to day.

I mean, they all had water and after the bloody bunny massacre from the other day, we knew they were being fed. And their cages were clean.

All of this surprised me, as I expected more . . . abuse?

"Do the tigers just leave you alone because they know you?" Ollie asked him with his bad French-American accent. I didn't bother stopping him in this case, because I doubted the man in front of us would be able to discern that his accent was mediocre at best.

Cap'n Bob let out a bark of a laugh.

"Are ye kidding? Those cats don't give two flying monkeys whether they know me or not," he said. "They would happily rip me apart if I got close enough."

Then, as if to illustrate his point, he took a step

toward one of the cages. Before I could even process what was happening, the tiger lunged at him.

"Morning, Ginger," Cap'n Bob said without missing a beat.

I looked over at Ollie, expecting him to continue his line of questioning but saw that he was frozen with fear.

If he didn't start snapping out of it, he wasn't going to be able to pull off his part of all this.

"Er, so how *do* you manage to get inside there without— in your words—*being ripped apart?*" I asked him.

"We take 'em out," Cap'n Bob said. "Let them hang tight for a few hours in one of these."

He pointed over to an even smaller cage, roughly the size of the tiger's body. It was sitting on top of a large wooden pallet. Attached to the flat board was a metal pallet truck that allowed the board—and anything on it—to be moved around with ease.

"All the cage doors open straight into the individual crates, so we don't have to get too close to the animals when transporting them," he said, showing us how it worked by sliding the crate door up into the air and then dropped it again like a guillotine.

"And they just go in willingly?" Ollie asked, seeming to find his voice again.

"For the most part," Cap'n Bob answered. "But for those who are more . . . stubborn, we sometimes throw a rat or two into the back of the receiving cage to get them moving."

"Do you ever sedate them?" I asked as we started to walk back the way we came.

Cap'n Bob kept his head down, but I saw him glance at me. "We can, and have. But I prefer not to drug 'em," he said slowly. "Do you know how hard it is to move a five-hundred-pound passed-out tiger? Dang near impossible."

"Fair enough," I said.

We were back at our golf cart, and I felt satisfied that we had everything we needed.

"Do you live on the grounds?" I asked Cap'n Bob. "So you can take care of the animals round the clock?"

Then he said the most peculiar thing.

"They don't pay me enough to live here," he said, a weird look on his face.

"So, nobody's watching the animals at night?" I asked, surprised.

Cap'n Bob swept his hands around. "They're not exactly going anywhere, are they?" he said.

I cocked my head to the side.

"Well, aren't you worried what would happen if they broke out?" I asked him curiously. "They could really hurt someone."

Cap'n Bob gave me a look I couldn't quite decipher, then nodded his head. "Now I suppose that they could," he said.

Then he turned around and walked away.

Entry Thirty-One

There were so many things to do before the dinner party, that I was running on empty by the time Thursday night rolled around.

"Yeah," I said into my phone and rubbing at my eyes. "That's right. Look, I really appreciate this. We wouldn't be able to pull this off without you."

I paused while the person spoke, but I was fading so fast that all I wanted to do was wrap it up. This call was the last one I needed to make before everything would be in place for the heist.

"Uh-huh. Yep. Okay, thanks again!" I said, trying to muster up one final burst of energy before passing out.

When I finally hit the End button on my phone I collapsed back onto my bed and closed my eyes.

I was already starting to drift off when I heard something at my door. The recognizable creaking it made when it was pushed open slightly.

Creeeeaaak. Creak, creak.

I didn't want to open my eyes.

So tired.

But what if it was a burglar?

Ha! I was too exhausted to even laugh out loud at the thought.

"Frankie?" came a voice, breaking through my sleepy haze.

"Mmmmm."

"Are you really asleep at . . . *seven thirty*?" Uncle Scotty asked. "Did you forget about movie night? I already made popcorn."

I sighed and opened my eyes.

"No," I said.

We'd made plans earlier that week to watch that movie of his with Johnny Depp and that awful song. If I canceled now, Uncle Scotty might suspect something was wrong, and I really didn't want him on my case now.

"I'll get up," I said finally.

"Great!" Uncle Scotty said, perking up. "Pizza's on the way, too!"

His glee over my response was obvious and I thought about how strange it was that someone who read people for a living would be so bad at hiding his own emotions.

"Awesome," I said, forcing myself to wake up. "I'll be down in a minute."

A short while later, we were downstairs in the living room with the movie rolling. Each of us had taken up an end of the couch, the pizza in between us—half pepperoni for Uncle Scotty and half chicken sausage, caramelized onions, and artichoke with a pesto sauce for me. The lights were low and the only sounds in the house were of us chewing and the beginning of a film Uncle Scotty swore was a classic.

"You've been pretty busy lately," Uncle Scotty said between bites. "Aren't you supposed to be on winter break?"

I took another bite and kept my eyes on the screen ahead.

"Hey, *you're* the one who insisted I go to that school," I argued. "The whole volunteering thing was *their* idea. You can blame them for my spotty attendance here."

"But you can't be spending *all* your time at The Farm. I know Kayla, and she wouldn't work you that hard," Uncle Scotty said slowly.

I shrugged my shoulders, staying noncommittal about it.

"So where have you been spending the rest of your time?" he asked like he wasn't digging.

"With Ollie," I said, not wanting to lie but obviously unable to tell him the whole truth.

"And how *is* Oliver doing?" Uncle Scotty asked. "I'm surprised he gave up the opportunity for popcorn and a movie."

"We're both a little spread thin these days," I said. "I think he just needed a night to rest."

I didn't mention that I hadn't invited him.

Not because I didn't want him there, but because I wanted him on his game for the heist. One of us had to be.

"I've never known Oliver to rest a day in his life,"

Uncle Scotty said, jokingly. "Is he finally sick of coming over here?"

I laughed. "Not even a little bit," I said. "He loves it over here. Probably more than he loves his own house. Though, I don't know why."

"The grass is always greener," Uncle Scotty said shrugging.

"But it's not," I said, sitting up straighter. "Did you know he lives in a mansion?"

Uncle Scotty looked surprised to learn this.

"Oliver?" he asked, curiously.

"Yeah," I said. "Weird, huh?

"It's a little—well, I wouldn't have guessed that, no," Uncle Scotty said. "What do his parents do?"

"That's the interesting thing," I said. "They don't *do* anything. They won the lottery and moved into their house the same month. Ollie thinks it's annoying because I guess their lives haven't changed much since they got the money. Except for maybe the fact that they're taking care of their extended family now too, and instead of being a landscaper for other rich families, his dad tends to his community garden and manages a dozen employees."

"Good for them," Uncle Scotty said, nodding. "They're being smart. Lotto money doesn't last forever."

"Ollie thinks they're being selfish by not spending all of it on designer clothes and his entertainment career."

"Oliver is a little dramatic sometimes," Uncle Scotty pointed out.

226

"Sometimes?" I asked, snorting.

"I was trying to be judicious," Uncle Scotty offered. "So, what does Oliver think of working at The Farm?"

"He likes it," I said, taking another bite of pizza. "But he thinks it's ruining his personal style—all the cat and dog hair and stuff. He's not so keen on picking up poop, either. Oh, and I guess he's also a little afraid of most of the animals. So . . . maybe he doesn't like it? I don't know. We both like Kayla though."

"You do?" Uncle Scotty asked, taking his eyes off the screen for a second to look over at me.

"Yeah," I said. "She's nice. Like a Disney princess. You can tell she really cares about the animals. And she never sugarcoats things just because we're kids. Treats us like we're her equals. Not a lot of adults do that."

"Is that a hint for me?" Uncle Scotty asked.

"No," I said, chuckling. "You're my uncle, so you've gotta be sort of parenty. Kayla's . . . just a girl to us. Like the big sister who we can go to for advice."

"You've needed advice lately?" Uncle Scotty asked, sounding interested.

"Not particularly," I said. "I'm just saying, if I *did* need advice, she's someone I feel like I could go to. You know, if I *wanted* that sort of thing."

I kept my focus on Johnny Depp even though I was no longer paying attention to the story. We stayed silent for a few seconds. Then Uncle Scotty cleared his throat.

"You can always come to me for advice too, you

know?" he said nonchalantly. "If you were looking for that sort of thing."

I tried to fight the smile but couldn't.

"I know, Uncle Scotty," I said.

"Like, for instance, if something had happened between you and your dad when you went to visit him, I would probably be in a unique position to understand what you're going through. You know, since he's my brother, and he's done things to piss me off too. I'm just saying . . . I could be a person you go to, to talk about that stuff. I promise not to be too—what did you call it? Too *parenty*."

I chuckled hearing my generally serious uncle use a completely made-up word just to get on my level.

It was sweet.

And it reminded me how cool he'd been through this whole thing. Other parents would have freaked if their kid suddenly cut off their hair and dyed it bright white. Uncle Scotty might've made a few comments, but not once had he tried to pry or tell me I shouldn't change my look.

That was when I realized that my uncle wasn't just someone I *could* go to for advice. He was someone I *wanted* to go to for advice. And I actually cared what he thought.

Whoa.

The realization shocked me to my core.

"You're right," I told him, surprising him, too. "Wanna give it a shot?"

I could see, even in the dark, that he was trying really

hard not to smile. And this made me smile. Finally he shrugged like it wasn't the big deal we both knew it was.

"Sure," he said.

"When I went to visit Dad, he told me he wanted me to be a normal kid." I said the words tentatively.

Uncle Scotty paused a moment before saying, "Wow." Then he took in a deep breath and let it out loudly. "That wasn't what I was expecting, but okay. Um, and that made you feel—"

It was a line straight from my therapist, but for some reason, it felt different coming from Uncle Scotty.

"Mad," I said quickly. "And maybe kind of . . . *not good enough*? Like, him saying he wanted me to be a normal kid, felt like he didn't want me to be . . . *me* anymore. Does that make any sense?"

Uncle Scotty was already nodding before I'd finished.

"Absolutely," he said and turned on the couch to face me. "You said you liked that Kayla didn't sugarcoat stuff, right? So, can I be brutally honest with you?"

Uh-oh. Maybe Uncle Scotty and I weren't ready for this just yet.

I swallowed.

"Please," I answered, though I was sort of dreading what he was about to say.

"Frankie, you have never been, nor will you ever be *normal*," he said bluntly.

This might've been an insult to about ninety-nine percent of the population, but to me, it was a compliment. And my uncle knew that.

"You might be able to fake it if you want to, but actually be a normal kid at your core? Yeah, not happening. Nor should it," he added at the end.

"Right?" I exclaimed, so happy to be talking to an adult who seemed to understand. "So why was he being such a jerk about it?"

Uncle Scotty paused here as he chose his next words carefully.

"Sometimes despite our best intentions, we, as human beings, aren't the greatest communicators," he started. "And as worldly as your dad is, he's still human, and he makes mistakes. I think he simply chose the wrong words to express what he really meant."

"He just kept telling me I should be normal, and be like the other kids my age," I said, frustrated.

"And what *you* heard was, 'You need to change who you are. You need to be different,'" Uncle Scotty said.

"Yeah," I answered quietly. "And I like who I am."

"I like who you are too," Uncle Scotty said. "Honestly, so does your dad. He's just scared that you'll follow in his footsteps instead of making your own way. I think that's the kind of change he meant. He just didn't know how to say it."

"I don't want to change who I am for anyone," I said quietly, feeling too tired to fight this battle right now.

"And you shouldn't," he answered. "You change for you, because *you* want to become a better version of yourself. And as incredible a kid you are, there's always room for improvement. As you get older, you'll start to realize that you want to do better. Be better. Make your mark on this world count. And you'll need to embrace change to do that. You can grow without losing yourself in the process."

I nodded because what he was saying made sense.

"Aw, crap," I said finally, dropping my hands down into my lap.

"What?" he asked, looking worried. "Was that too parenty?"

"No," I said with a sigh. "It was perfect."

"And that makes you mad because . . . ," he asked, confused now.

"Because now I have to apologize to Dad," I said.

Uncle Scotty smiled as I got up from the couch and walked toward the stairs tiredly.

"Hey, Frankie?" he said, stopping me before I disappeared.

"Yeah?"

"You don't have to apologize right away," he said with a smile. "Your dad can probably stand to stew a little bit. Might even be good for him."

I grinned back.

"Now *that's* good advice," I said before heading upstairs to bed.

Entry Thirty-Two

Heading into the twins' dinner party that night alone, felt a bit like walking into the jungle.

I'll never admit it to him, but I would've felt better having Ollie with me. But for our plan to work, he couldn't be here. He needed to be at the zoo.

And bit or not, it was the safer of the two locations.

Before going inside, I pressed the button on my earpiece and talked softly to myself.

"Ollie, what's your status?" I asked.

After a few seconds of silence, I heard his side crackle and then he started to talk.

"Sorry, still getting used to this whole *Mission Impossible* ear-thingy, which, by the way, is freaking awesome," he said.

"Focus, Ollie," I reminded him, but smiled under the glow of the entranceway.

"Right," he said, pulling it together. "So, got here fine. The back guard barely looked at me as I came through. The grounds are quiet. Well, the tigers keep growling at me, but besides that, it's quiet. And dark. And creepy, if I'm being honest. Just waiting for your guy to show, and we can start whenever you give us the go-ahead."

"Good," I said, happy to hear things were going smoothly on his end. "Hang tight and be safe."

"That's the plan," he answered, and then the line went silent again.

I took a deep breath and then pushed open the front door.

It wasn't difficult to follow the sound of the party out to the terrace. Glowing lanterns had been set up all around, giving the space a fun, festive flair. And with all the lights shining, you could barely see the eyesore of a construction site just beyond the celebration.

Tables had been set up, and pristine white tablecloths covered each. Waiters walked around filling glasses with champagne and offering hors d'oeuvres, while music played softly in the background.

When I'd originally heard "dinner party" I thought there'd be maybe ten guests.

I was wrong.

There were about thirty people here.

And they all looked rich.

"Okay," I said, adjusting the gown I'd worn for the night and then tipping my chin into the air. If I was going to fit in with this crowd, I had to exude a certain amount of confidence, superiority, and arrogance that came with wealth and power.

I had to walk in like everyone here should be honored that I showed up.

With that in mind, I began to strut around like I owned the place.

I said hello to guests as if *they* should know who I was.

Heads began to turn toward me and I acted like the attention meant nothing.

And then I walked straight up to Emma and Sam, who were standing in the center of a small group of people.

"*Bonsoir, mes amis,*" I said, interrupting a woman with short red hair midsentence. I leaned in and gave Emma a kiss on each cheek, and then greeted Sam the same way. "I'm sorry I'm late."

"Not at all," Emma cooed, before turning back to the group. "Everyone, this is Brigeet. She is the editor-in-chief of *French Fur* magazine. The magazine is doing an in-depth feature on us for an upcoming issue. Brigeet is also a new *collaborator* of ours. I'm sure you'll all get to know each other better in the months to come."

I nodded at everyone.

"Brigeet, this is Geo Ford," Sam said, introducing me to an older man with silver hair.

The eccentric billionaire who wanted to hunt tigers for fun.

"*Bonjour,*" I said.

You vile excuse for a human being.

"And this is Thoya Vanderhook," Emma said, motioning to a stunning blond woman standing next to an equally stunning blond man.

The supermodel turned designer.

"*Un plaisir,*" I said, holding out my hand to her.

234

A pleasure—to bring you down.

Then Emma and Sam introduced me to some of the others.

There was a member of the Mexican consulate. A titan of industries. The creator of some app. A socialite. A famous actor—the one you're always reading about in the tabloids.

There were others, but they all started to blend together for me. Besides, I wasn't really there to network. I was there to bring them down.

After we'd been seated for dinner—I found my name-plate nestled in between a former NFL quarterback and a YouTube influencer—I waited for the speech Emma and Sam gave welcoming everyone. And then right as the appetizer was being served, I excused myself to use the restroom.

Not that anyone was paying any attention to me anymore.

Fancy food tended to distract people rather effectively.

Slipping out of the formal dining room, I headed in the direction of the bathroom, but sailed right past it. Instead, I tiptoed down the hallway, noting Emma's meditation room on my right and continuing on until I got to the end of the hall.

I stopped abruptly in front of the entrance to the Jungle Room.

With a quick look behind me to make sure nobody was coming, out of my sleeve I pulled the key Emma had been wearing earlier that evening and stuck it in the lock. It had been easy to take it from her—I'd simply cut the string from around her neck while embracing before sitting down for dinner. I planned to drop it back down by her chair when I was finished using it so she didn't notice it had been gone.

Before turning the key, I punched in the six numbers I'd memorized after seeing Emma unlock the door before. I wasn't sure if she was just super trusting or she assumed I wouldn't dare read the numbers over her shoulder, but Emma might as well have just handed me the code.

With a deep breath, I turned the key and pushed open the door.

The hallway appeared empty. But I knew what was hidden from eye's view. Taking the bag I'd stashed behind a plant earlier in the week, I retrieved my own pair of glasses that would allow me to see the lasers. Slipping them on, I was surprised once again by the elaborate labyrinth of red beams filling the room.

I'd always known that snagging Emma's key would be an easy grab for me—people thought that placing something on their person kept it safe, but it just wasn't true. Not for a seasoned thief at least.

That said, I hadn't been confident that I'd *also* have the time and opportunity to steal her phone, too, that operated the lasers.

So, in the end, I'd decided I'd just have to go old-school with the lasers, and navigate them.

Just inside the door, I pulled my dress up and over my head, revealing the full body suit I was wearing underneath. I placed my heels and dress on the floor near the door and then slipped my hands through the straps of my backpack and secured it to my body.

Turning once again to the hallway of lasers, I began to chart my path to the other side. During my first heist, I'd only had to worry about lasers that hovered just above the floor. Here, they weaved around the whole room, which would take far more planning and care.

Like a chess player, I worked out my path ahead of time before approaching the first beam.

Then I took a step. Right over that first red line. Followed by a crouching position with one leg extended out to the side, before rolling my body down toward the floor, almost brushing it with my stomach in the process.

I dove over the next one, curling my chin toward my chest as I performed a forward roll.

But as I went to stand up, I realized I'd built up too much momentum and started to fall toward the next set of lasers. I sucked in my stomach and managed to stop a quarter of an inch away from the alarm.

I didn't breathe again until I'd settled back onto my heels, my balance fully intact. When I was sure I was steady, I looked at the next batch of red lights. They were all so close together that it would be impossible for me to get through.

At least from the ground.

Luckily, I'd prepared for this.

I pulled out the grappling hook launcher—the same one we'd used on my first heist—and held it overhead. It made a *pooft* sound as it sprang up toward the ceiling, and then there was a satisfying *crunch* as the contraption embedded itself into the drywall.

"She shoots, she scores!" I whispered, then breathed out loudly mimicking a roaring crowd.

I chuckled to myself.

Dad would've loved that.

But Dad wasn't here.

I was.

And so was Ollie.

Ollie!

I touched my earbud.

"You there?" I asked Ollie.

"Who is this?" Ollie asked.

I rolled my eyes as I pulled hard on the rope that now hung from the ceiling, making sure it would hold my weight.

"Very funny," I said unenthusiastically.

Ollie chuckled. "What's up, Buttercup?"

I paused.

"I told you that's not going to be my call sign," I said.

"Well, I'm not calling you Master of the Universe," he argued.

"Why not?" I asked jokingly. "It fits."

Ollie snorted.

"What do you want?" he asked finally.

"Just checking in," I said, attaching two handheld grappling hooks to my belt.

These weren't just plain old grappling hooks though. These were souped-up grappling hooks that Dad and I had commissioned from one of the best gadget guys in the industry to create. As far as I knew, only four were ever made.

Dad had two.

At least he had at one point.

They might actually be in some government building, inside an evidence bag somewhere right now.

The important thing was, I had the other two.

"Your *little surprise* got here about fifteen minutes ago and now we're just working out logistics," Ollie said. "He's a pretty cool dude. Bat-crap crazy, but cool."

I laughed.

"Sounds about right," I said, climbing up the rope until I was just inches away from the ceiling.

I retrieved one of the grappling hooks from my belt and slipped the handle between my fingers and gripped it a couple times in my hand.

Oh, how I've missed you.

Then, I leaned out and placed the device up against the ceiling a foot away from me. I pressed the green button on the handle and felt the grappling prongs spring out and attach themselves to the ceiling. Slowly, I lowered my body until I was hanging from the device.

A foot above the alarms.

"What are you up to?" Ollie asked me, like this was a normal phone call.

"Oh, you know," I said, glancing up as I took the other hook and held it out in front of me and embedded it in the ceiling as well. "Just hanging around."

"Cool," Ollie said.

Suddenly there was the sound of commotion in the background where Ollie was. At first I figured it was just the typical noise that came along with transferring wild animals into new cages.

I was wrong.

"What are you doing here?" a gruff voice said loudly. "Who are you?"

There was shouting, some scuffling, and then static as Ollie's line went dead.

Entry Thirty-Three

"Ollie!" I shouted frantically. "What's happening? Freaking answer me!"

After twenty agonizing seconds, the other line crackled back to life and I could hear Ollie breathing hard.

"Ollie?" I asked, my heart hammering in my chest. "Was that . . . Cap'n Bob?"

Somehow I'd managed to keep my grip on the hooks during all of this, and was still hanging—shaking now—from the ceiling.

"Frankie?" Ollie asked, sounding far away.

The relief I felt was almost electric.

"Ollie!" I exclaimed. "Are you okay?"

"Yeah, I'm fine," Ollie said, still breathing hard.

"What happened? Did Cap'n Bob show up? He wasn't supposed to be on the grounds at night."

"Well, he was tonight," Ollie muttered under his breath.

"I can be to you in ten," I said, looking back the way I'd just come.

"No," Ollie said quickly. I could tell he'd had to force himself to say it. "No, let me handle this. You just focus on getting the stuff there."

"Are you sure? I can always come back here later—" I started.

"No, you can't," Ollie said. "You know you've only got a certain amount of time before somebody comes looking for you. This is *my* job and I'll take care of it."

"But—" I began to argue.

"Trust me with this, okay, Frankie?" he said, sounding very un-Ollie-like.

"Okay," I said with a grunt as I pulled the hook in my back hand out of the drywall and swung forward, attaching it in front of me. As I picked up momentum, it looked a bit like I was swinging across monkey bars.

Disconnect the back hook, swing, connect to the ceiling in the front. Disconnect the back hook, swing, connect to the ceiling in the front.

"Call me if you need me then," I said, nervous that Ollie was in over his head.

That we both were.

"Will do," he said to me.

After that, his side of the mic went flat.

When I finally reached the other side, I swung back and forth a few times before releasing the handheld hooks and dropping to the floor in a crouching position, the devices still in my hands.

I wanted to stress over what was going on with Ollie, but I couldn't do anything about it here. So, I turned my focus back to what I could control.

And I pushed open the Jungle Room door.

The whole room was dark, with the exception of some glowing orbs located strategically around the space. Each one was a different color and cast an almost eerie tone across the room.

"Grrrrrr." a tiny growl escaped one of the baby tigers.

My head swung in the direction of the sound and I was relieved to see that all four of the cats were locked inside their cages.

"Good kitties," I said quietly as I crossed the room to the glass aquarium that held the anaconda.

I pushed through the plants that hid most of the snake's habitat and peered inside. All I saw were large branches and logs, some rocks, a lot of foliage and— there! A flash of moving yellow back in the corner.

I began to make my way down the length of the enclosure, pushing aside plants to try to find the entrance to the snake cage. When I finally found it, I hesitated.

Was I really going in there with a twelve-foot-long anaconda?

Just as I was contemplating this, the snake slithered up, appeared to climb the side of the glass and looked straight at me. And then its tongue darted in and out like it could taste my fear.

I swear, it was saying, *Come on in. I promisssssssse I'll be nice.*

Yeah, right.

Then, just to the side of the snake, I noticed something else. Something that was even more incredible than the creature in front of me.

It was green and sparkled in the light and was the size of a stamp.

Holy crap.

I leaned forward and smacked my forehead against the glass clumsily.

"Ow!" I exclaimed, pulling back and rubbing my head.

I leaned in again, slower this time and tried to see through the fog my breath was making on the glass.

That was an emerald.

A huge emerald.

One that had to be worth a small fortune.

I turned my head a few inches farther to the right and saw a crystal clear diamond roughly the same size. And then another. And another.

Smaller gems littered the bottom of the cage as if they were pebbles on a beach.

Yep, I was definitely going in there.

While I'd been taking stock in the millions of dollars' worth of rocks inside the tank, the anaconda had continued to move around its cage. The snake's head was now about five feet away from the entrance, and I felt like that had to be far enough for me to do what I had to do next.

I pushed the large handle upward in a semicircular

motion until I heard it click and felt the door give just a little.

My eyes never left the snake and I breathed in relief as it didn't seem to react at all to the noise.

"Good girl," I said quietly. "Nothing to see here. Just keep slithering."

As I continued to talk to it, I pulled out a pre-filled needle, popped off the top with my teeth and spit it out on the floor next to me. I tapped the side to make sure no air was trapped, watched as a tiny bit squirted out, and then sunk the inch-long tip through the snake's tough skin.

If the anaconda felt it, she didn't act like it. Just went on her way, moving around the tank like nothing was different.

I closed up the door again and stood there, my hand on the glass as I watched her.

From what I'd learned at The Farm (a lot of the animals showed up beyond freaked out and often needed some help relaxing) it could take up to fifteen minutes for a tranquilizer and sleeping agent to fully kick in. Until then, I just had to wait.

I touched my earpiece.

"Ollie, you there?" I asked. "What's going on?"

Nothing.

"Ollie? Is everything all right with Cap'n Bob?"

All I got from the other side was silence.

Butterflies began to move around in my stomach.

I hadn't felt great about leaving Ollie to deal with the crisis on his own. And now that he wasn't answering, I wished I would've listened to my gut and abandoned this mission to save his.

I contemplated leaving right then, but the logical side of me knew it would be pointless. If Ollie had been caught, then we weren't going to get the animals out. Not tonight, at least. And I wasn't going to change that by charging in there after the fact. At least if I finished what I was doing here, we'd have money to do some good when this was all over.

I turned my focus back to the yellow creature in front of me. She'd stopped moving as far as I could tell and a clear film had covered her eyes. Since snakes didn't have eyelids, they couldn't close their eyes when they slept, but the film of skin shaded their corneas when they did.

Thank you, Animal Planet, for that nice little tidbit of information.

I took a deep breath, prayed that the snake was completely knocked out, and then opened the door. As I lifted my leg up and into the tank, I resisted the urge to run in the other direction.

You can do this. She's asleep. You have ten minutes and a job to do. Suck it up. Put your big-girl pants on. What would Veronica Mars do?

I placed my foot down onto the bottom of the enclosure, wincing as a crunching sound seemed to echo all around me. Before I could talk myself out of it, I pulled my other foot inside and started to move.

I headed right for the ginormous emerald I'd seen before. Plucking it from the ground, I squinted as I looked more closely at the jewel. It was beautiful. Unlike anything I'd ever seen in real life before. And it was about to be mine.

I threw it up in the air and caught it again in my palm before shoving it into a hidden pocket that had been sewn into the lining of my catsuit. I could see the lump when I looked down at myself, but since the material was black, nobody would be able to notice it from far away.

Then I began collecting other diamonds off the floor. There were dried-up piles of snake poop all over, but I didn't care. What was a little poop for millions of dollars in diamonds and gems?

I stuffed the jewels into my suit until I couldn't fit any more.

Then I turned to the wall safe.

And saw that the anaconda was curled up right in front of it.

She still appeared to be fast asleep, but I was going to have to step over her in order to get to whatever was inside, and the thought was terrifying.

Not that snakes grossed me out. I'd handled the boa in Kayla's office like a pro. But one this size could very well squeeze me to death or take a chomp of me with its razor-sharp fangs.

Neither of those possibilities sounded fun to me and I wanted to avoid it if I could help it.

"Okay," I said to the snake as I moved toward her. "Nice snake. Please don't wake up. Just stay asleep. I promise I won't bother you."

Even if she couldn't understand me, I felt a little better saying it.

I walked tentatively up to the snake and hesitated briefly before stepping over the first section of her body.

Crunch.

I froze and prayed she wouldn't move.

After a few harrowing seconds, I could see that she still wasn't moving, so I kept going.

Step, pause, wait. Step, pause, wait. Step, pause, wait.

When I finally reached the safe, I looked down at my feet and saw that I would have to straddle the area of the snake that was thickest in order to get to it. If the anaconda woke up and decided to wrap herself around my leg, it would be over for me before I even realized what was happening.

But, then—there was the safe.

And whatever treasures were inside.

My curiosity won out and I positioned my legs on either side of the snake, and then carefully leaned forward and reached up to the metal door handle. Digging into my backpack, I withdrew a velvet pouch and then carefully pulled the rare earth magnet out and held it up to admire it. This hockey-puck-size magnet could open up just about anything that had a metal lever. So, I tossed it into a tube sock and started moving it around the surface to find the lock. When I finally did, I dragged the magnet to the left and then pulled on the handle.

It opened with very little fanfare.

But what was inside was exciting enough.

Stacks and stacks of paper.

Paper money.

I'd handled enough money to recognize that each bundle inside was equal to $100,000. And there were more of these than I could count. I started to stuff the money into my backpack but as I emptied out the safe, I noticed something else in there, too.

A notebook.

What was a notebook doing inside a safe?

I pulled it out slowly and turned to the first page.

"Oh, mama," I said quietly as I began to flip through the whole thing. "Hello, little black book."

It was Emma and Sam's ledger of every deal and transaction they'd ever carried out. It listed each client by name, what they'd hired them for, and how much they'd been paid for their services.

All of the people listed were rich and powerful.

And the things the twins had done for them included far more than just procuring them exotic wild animals. In fact, the things recorded within those pages would send a lot of people away for a long time.

Somehow I'd stumbled upon the Holy Grail.

"Can you believe it?" I asked the enormous snake at my feet, glancing down like it was going to respond.

And when I did, I dropped the ledger. Then all the blood drained from my body.

The snake was awake.

"Well, aren't you a brave girl," a voice said from across the room.

I looked up, a strangled scream threatening to escape, as a pissed-off Emma strutted toward me.

Entry Thirty-Four

"Fool me once, shame on you," Emma said as she took slow, calculated steps toward me, her flowing gown trailing behind her.

"Fool you twice," I responded. "Shame on . . . well, *you* again."

"You probably think you're *so* clever," Emma said, walking up to the closest cat cage and unlocking it grandly. As she walked away, she swung the door open.

"Well, I don't suck, if that's what you mean," I said, the words coming out more bravely than I felt.

Inside I was panicking.

Without taking my eye off of Emma, I could feel the anaconda start to move at my feet. Its thick skin brushed up against my leg as it slithered around.

If it wrapped itself around my leg, I was a goner. I knew Emma wouldn't help me get out of here—not at this point—and anacondas were known for squeezing the life out of their prey. Not to mention the possibility of being bit by her.

I was trying to ignore that part completely.

I had to get out of here.

Moving at a pace that would practically pass as slow

motion, I grabbed my backpack and the ledger I had dropped. Then I picked up my leg, trying not to jostle the snake too much before stepping down on the other side of it.

This time, the crunching sound my shoes made against the debris was enough to cause the snake to turn and look right at me.

Emma clapped her hands together gleefully. "I knew we were having dinner tonight. I didn't know we were getting a show, too!"

She walked up to a second cat cage and unlocked it, too, leaving the baby tiger to escape on its own.

"Glad I could oblige," I said through clenched teeth as I took another slow step toward the open cage door.

The anaconda swayed from side to side with every movement I made. We were both equal distance from the opening, and if the snake got there before me, I'd be cornered inside.

"In the left corner, we have Brigeet, weighing in at roughly, what? Practically nothing?" Emma said, making her voice sound like an announcer's as she let a third tiger out of its cage. "And on the right, we have Julia, the yellow anaconda, who weighs three times as much as her opponent."

Taking another careful step, I watched as the snake moved closer, too.

"You named a snake *Julia*?" I asked, snorting.

"It's my grandmother's name," she answered, annoyed as she freed the last tiger. They were all roaming around the room now, a fact that didn't seem to bother Emma at all, but worried me greatly.

She'd been wrong when she'd called me brave before. She was the brave one.

Or stupid.

At this point, an argument could be made for both.

"If I were your grandma, I'd be pissed," I said.

"Oh, she is," Emma said, flippantly. "Or was. She's dead now."

"Die of disappointment, did she?" I asked. I knew it was cruel, but I had to keep her off-balance until I could get out of here.

"No," Emma said bluntly. "Snake bite."

My head snapped up and I stopped midstride.

"Wait, seriously?" I asked.

Emma paused. Then she started to laugh. It was beyond creepy. Her face had gone from its usual laid-back zen to looking almost maniacal. Her eyes were wide, the pupils dilated, and parts of her hair had broken free of her chic updo.

"No," she admitted. "But you're about to experience it yourself."

I glanced over at Julia. She was full-on agitated now. I wasn't sure if it was because the medicine was on its way out of her system and she was fully waking up or if she was bothered by the fact that I was invading her space.

As I watched, she slithered back and forth, a predator pacing before striking its prey.

I had to move. And fast.

I figured my best option was to make a run for it. I might not make it out of the tank without being attacked, but it was the only thing that offered me even a chance of staying alive.

"Don't count me out just yet," I said, and took a running leap toward the tank door.

As I soared through the air, arms fully outstretched in front of me, I caught a flash of yellow out of the corner of my eye.

I didn't even have time to yell out as it sunk its fangs into my leg.

"Awww, so close," Emma said, snapping her fingers like she actually cared.

I landed with the top half of my body leaning out of the tank and hanging down toward the floor. Before I could assess how hurt I was, I dragged myself the rest of the way out and crumbled into a heap below

"How you doin' over there?" Emma called out, absolutely zero concern in her voice.

I couldn't see her from where I'd landed, the foliage was just too thick. But that worked out in my favor.

I didn't want her to see me struggle if this was the end.

But she'd asked a good question.

How *was* I?

I rolled over onto my back and slowly lifted my leg into the air so I could assess the damage. It certainly hurt. Felt like I'd been stabbed in the calf.

With a hundred forks.

But as I inspected my lower half, I saw that the snake's many teeth—anacondas had four rows of backward-facing fangs up top, two on the bottom—had failed to break through my jumpsuit and puncture my skin.

I ran my hand along the material and let out a shaky breath.

Thank gosh I'd spent the extra money to have my outfit made out of Kevlar. The special material was supposed to stop a bullet, so my theory had been that maybe it'd give me some protection from fangs.

Cat or snake.

So far, so good.

"Are you alive?" Emma called out. "If you aren't, it'd save me a lot of time and hassle. Groan if you're still conscious."

I rolled my eyes.

"You're out of luck," I called.

"Poo!" Emma said back. "Oh, well. Destroying you myself will be fun, too."

My adrenaline started up again as her threat sunk in. Before I'd seen that ledger, I wouldn't have thought she was capable of murder. Sure, she'd done some awful things, but killing someone seemed like something on a whole other level.

But now . . .

I knew that wasn't true. And I needed to get out of here alive so I could make it back to Ollie.

Ollie.

He was still out there, waiting for my go-ahead. That is, if Cap'n Bob hadn't shut him down already.

"Ollie," I whispered into my ear piece.

Come on, come on, come on.

The line crackled to life. "Yeah, what's up?"

"You good?" I asked quietly.

I heard a loud roar in the background and my heart seized.

"As good as I can be surrounded by enormous beasts who look at me like I'm a giant hot dog," he said.

"Good," I whispered, not having the energy to laugh at his joke. "Go ahead and get going."

"Will do," he said. "And you'll be along soon?"

"I'll leave here as soon as I can," I promised. "But if I'm not there in fifteen, go without me. I'll catch up with you later."

The truth was, I had no idea when I'd be out of here.

If I'd get out of here.

"Oh, Brigeeeeeet!" Emma called out breezily. "I have a party to get back to. Be a doll and come out here so I can feed you to my kitties."

I began to sweat as I thought about the not-exactly-small cats roaming around just feet away from me. Running my hands along my legs, I felt the toughness of the material. The fang-proof catsuit had worked once, but I had no idea how much it could ultimately withstand.

I had to come to terms with the idea that I might not

get out of here. Not as planned at least. And if that was the case, I needed to make sure all of this wasn't for nothing. I had to get proof to the rest of the world that Emma and Sam were bad guys.

But how?

Suddenly I remembered I had something else in my bag of tricks that would ensure none of this would go unknown.

I pulled the tiny microphone out of my backpack and turned the battery pack to the On position. I'd found the body mic on a table earlier that night—Emma or Sam must have discarded it there after forgetting to take it off again—and I had snatched it up on a whim.

Now I was so glad I had.

I lay the rest of my gear down on the ground and then stood up with my backpack on, brushing myself off, and shaking the fear away.

Then I stepped out from the cover of trees and plants and into Emma's view.

"Ahhh, there you are," she said, standing between me and the only way out of the room. Her arms were folded across her chest like she was annoyed that I'd kept her waiting. "I was hoping Julia had gobbled you up after all."

"Sorry to disappoint," I answered. Then I thought about it. "Well, actually—sorry, not sorry."

"Watch your mouth," Emma warned me dangerously. She leaned down to pet one of the cats that was weaving in and out of her legs. There were a few cats to the right of me, too, getting closer than I would prefer. "Or this little guy might just rip that tongue out."

She said this like she was talking to a baby, which made the sentence doubly creepy. I acted like it didn't bother me, even though inside it made me shudder.

"But then I won't be able to answer all the questions you have for me," I said instead, placing my hands under the straps of my backpack casually. "You *do* have questions, don't you?"

I was counting on her curiosity to get the best of her, and after a few moments of silence, she finally shrugged and gave in.

"Okay, I'll bite," Emma said. "You're clearly not a magazine editor—or from France, since your accent has mysteriously disappeared—so who are you really?"

I raised my eyebrow. It hadn't been a conscious decision to let my real voice come out. More like, I had more important things occupying my mind than continuing the ruse.

Oh, well. It's not like it would *really* give me away or anything.

"I'm just a girl," I said easily. "Just a *normal* girl who's *really* good at bringing down people like you."

"People like *us*?" Emma asked, confused.

"You know, bad guys," I said simply.

Emma snorted.

"And what makes us *so* bad?" she asked me seriously.

I blinked at her in response.

Was she really that clueless?

"Um, you're rich, powerful, heartless, cruel, callous, conniving, despicable," I said, ticking off each point with my fingers. "Did I leave anything out? Oh, yeah, you're *murderers*."

Emma waved this off like I was overexaggerating.

"It's not murder if they were gonna die anyway," Emma argued. "Besides, considering who the animals might've gone to live with, I was probably doing them a favor. Did you hear what Ford wants to do with his tigers? People can be so sick."

"Hello, pot, meet kettle," I said, amazed by the depth of her denial. Then I shook my head. "You supply your friends with endangered, exotic animals, knowing full well that they're going to live painful, sad, miserable lives. That's if they live at all. How do you sleep at night?"

Emma laughed at this and gestured around the room.

"I sleep on thousand-dollar sheets. I'm doing just fine," she retorted. "And I'm bored of you now. Time to give these little ones a treat."

Emma walked over to a mini-fridge in the corner and pulled out a Tupperware container filled with something dark. As she walked closer to me, I could see that it was full of something red and juicy.

"They don't always get filet mignon, but tonight's special," she said. Then she put her finger up to her mouth and whispered. "Don't tell them, but it's sort of their last meal. Thanks to a lucrative deal I just made during the salad course, these babies just got a new home."

"You're disgusting," I spat, unable to believe someone as vile as her existed.

She opened up the container and threw several hunks of meat at me.

"Who's disgusting now?" she answered.

I would've rolled my eyes at the lame comeback but the tigers had already smelled the steak and were heading right for me.

I glanced back to try to find any way I could escape the oncoming slaughter. But I wasn't about to climb back into the snake cage. That was almost worse than taking my chance with the baby tigers.

"You're really going to feed me to your tigers?" I asked her, remembering that the microphone was recording our conversation.

I looked down and saw that one of the cats was actually going for a piece of meat that had landed on my shoe. I kicked it off and the cat ran after it. The others were still chowing down right in front of me and I knew it was just a matter of time before they decided they wanted me as their main course.

"Sorry, not sorry," Emma said back to me, making a face. "God, that phrase is just so annoy—"

Penelope leaped onto Emma from behind, knocking the words right out of her mouth, and her to the ground. As she fell, her head bounced off the floor and then she went still.

I was too startled to even scream.

The tiger walked right over her owner's body and began to lick the empty Tupperware container that had flown out of Emma's hands when she'd been tackled.

"Emma," I said tentatively.

Another cat lunged at my foot, and before I could give it much thought, I kicked the remaining meat as far away from me as possible. The cats ran after it instinctually and I walked slowly over to Emma, who still hadn't moved.

I kicked the Tupperware away and watched as Penelope followed it too, and then joined her brothers in the opposite corner where the meat was quickly being devoured. Leaning down, I felt Emma's neck for a pulse.

And breathed a sigh of relief.

It was still there.

I stood back up and looked over at the exit, and then back down at Emma. As awful as she was, I couldn't leave her to the tigers.

I wasn't a bad guy.

But I wasn't about to give her another chance to stop me either.

I glanced around and when my eyes fell onto one of the empty cages, it was like fate had intervened.

I grabbed underneath Emma's arms and dragged her over to the closest cage and locked her inside.

There. She was safe *and* locked up.

Just like she should be.

Next, I turned to the baby tigers. I couldn't leave them roaming around here either. Not when the people at the dinner party probably wanted to make them into stuffed animals or something.

I'd decided to get all the exotics out, and that's what I was going to do.

Hopefully I'd be able to do it without losing any limbs in the process.

Thinking quickly, I scanned the room for something I could use as a lure. There was a stuffed animal, torn and frayed, lying on top of the ottoman that would work perfectly. I retrieved it and took some rope from my bag and tied it around the doll. Finally, I reached back inside for a bottle of amber liquid.

Calvin Klein's Obsession.

I made a face before popping off the top and dumping it all over the stuffed toy. Then I tossed the empty bottle across the room.

"Here kitty, kitty, kitty," I said, swinging the rope with the perfume-soaked toy attached over to the tigers.

I hadn't totally believed it when I'd read about it online, but seeing their reaction was unreal. As soon as the cats caught a whiff of the popular perfume, they went nuts. Rolling over it, licking it, nuzzling the doll. Apparently, the musky scent was like catnip for them.

I pulled the rope cautiously and watched as the baby tigers began to follow it.

"Okay cubbies, time to escape this place," I said, leading them out of the Jungle Room and into the main house.

Entry Thirty-Five

I doubt Calvin Klein had this in mind when he made his perfume.

I dragged the stuffed animal behind me at a slow pace through the mansion halls, the cats staying on course every step of the way.

It had smelled great the first few minutes, but after several yards, my head started to swim and I was developing a headache.

But the cats loved it.

And if it meant being able to get them—and me—out safely, I'd happily endure the pain.

I lead the cats into the main entryway of the house, their big paws click-clacking across the marble floors. I could hear the noise coming from the dinner party and prayed that nobody left at this exact moment to use the restroom.

I could lie my way out of it, but it would cost me valuable time that I didn't have.

I didn't breathe again until I slipped out the back door, the tigers all in tow, and made it down to my golf cart. Climbing into the driver's seat, I quickly tied the long rope to the back and then started the engine.

I took one final look at the house as the rumbling sound of the vehicle rang out in the night, and said a silent goodbye to everyone inside.

Not that I cared to ever see any of them again.

Then I started to drive.

The cats were fast. Michaela had said that tigers could run up to forty miles per hour. I had the cart cranked up as fast as it would go and the cubs had no problem keeping up.

I might've been imagining it, but it looked like they were having fun.

And why wouldn't they?

They were free.

We all were.

I pulled Emma's cell out of my pocket and dialed 911. She'd dropped it when Penelope had jumped her, and I'd picked it up on our way out of the Jungle Room.

"Hello, nine-one-one, what's your emergency?" the woman's voice said on the other end of the line.

"I'm at a dinner party at the Brasko estate and they have all these exotic animals running around," I said frantically in my French-American accent. "The woman of the house, Emma, is unconscious. Please send help right away. Oh, and the FBI might be especially interested in seeing what's hidden in the snake's cage."

"And what is your name—" the operator began, but I hung up and tossed the phone into some bushes.

The scent of the perfume wafted behind the vehicle as

I drove, and the cats eagerly followed. When I saw the zoo up ahead, I couldn't hold back my smile.

It was almost over.

Ollie turned to look at me as I drove up. It must've been quite a sight: a tiny girl driving a golf cart, followed by four large baby tigers who were obsessed with trying to get a stuffed animal that was tied to the back of my seat.

When I pulled up to where Ollie was standing, my friend just shook his head.

"You had to make an entrance, didn't you?" Ollie said sarcastically.

"You're just jealous you don't have tigers following *you* around," I said, getting out of the vehicle.

"True," he admitted.

Then he glanced around to the back of the cart and watched as the tigers attacked the stuffed animal with fervor, now that the vehicle had stopped.

"Actually, I'm okay with it," he said. "You can be the mother of tigers."

A figure stepped out into the light then and a grin spread across my face.

"Angus!" I said, running up to him and jumping up to give him a hug.

"Lass!" he said, talking in my wig as he swung me around. "Well, aren't you a sight!"

"Why, thank you!" I said, posing like a superhero after he put me down.

"I can't believe how much you've grown," he said, placing his hand over his mouth in disbelief. "You're like, a *real* kid now."

"Um, hate to break it to you, but I've always been a real kid," I said, laughing.

"Ye know what I mean," he said, his Scottish accent coming out heavy, just like I remembered it. "Yer all grown."

"Can you tell my dad that?" I asked, smiling. Then I turned back to Ollie who appeared to be enjoying our exchange. "You two have met, I take it?"

Angus nodded and walked over to my friend. When he clapped Ollie on the back, he was thrust forward clumsily.

"Aye. Ye picked a good partner here, ye have," Angus said cheerily as Ollie beamed from the compliment.

Then, when Ollie wasn't looking, Angus leaned in to me and added under his breath, "A little theatrical for me tastes, but he gets the job done."

I watched Angus as he walked over to the baby tigers. He picked up the stuffed animal and made a face as he smelled the perfume, then tossed the whole thing into an empty cage. The four cubs rushed in after it and the door clanged down behind them.

"Well, that was easy," he said, shrugging before motioning for a few of the other guys to load them up.

I began to giggle. I couldn't help it. I'd made it out of the Jungle Room alive, I'd gotten the tiger cubs to safety without being eaten, and my best friend and former co-thief were both here with me. All we had to do now was get in the waiting trucks and get out of here before the cops showed up. . . .

Suddenly though, I remembered something that made me freeze.

"Wait, what happened with Cap'n Bob?" I asked, looking around frantically.

"He nearly called the cops on you for not bringing him in on the plan earlier," Cap'n Bob's gruff voice said from behind me.

I jumped as I turned around to find the older man limping toward me, his usual scowl on his face.

"How do you always do that?" I asked him, frustrated. "Sneak up on people."

"What yer really askin' is how I can sneak up on you with me bum leg?" he said bluntly.

"I wasn't!" I exclaimed, even though I'd been thinking it. And then since he'd brought it up, I added, "Was it an animal bite?"

Cap'n Bob nodded. "But not one of these," he said, nodding at the trucks. "This was from a great white."

"A shark?" I asked, surprised.

"Aye," he said. "Why do ya think they call me Cap'n?"

"I always thought it was cuz you were *captain of this ship*," Ollie chimed in, making quotation motions with his hands.

Cap'n Bob burst into raucous laughter.

"Now that's a good one!" he said, his whole body

shaking. "Nah, I was a ship's captain in my previous life. Couldn't sail no more with this leg, so ended up here."

"Speaking of," I segued. "We figured you'd be loyal to the Braskos since you work for them. Why did you help us?"

Cap'n Bob snorted.

"I ain't loyal to no one except these animals," he said, jutting his chin out defiantly. "And the Braskos don't care about me, let alone any of 'em."

"Oh," I said. "Well, thank you. Honestly, this could've all gone badly if you weren't here to help."

"Anything to get these critters away from here," he said. "I'd have done it myself if I had the connections you do."

"Well, we're very grateful," I said, beginning to walk away. But then I thought of something and turned back. "You know, I might have a job for you after this."

I could hear sirens in the distance and looked around at all the empty cages.

"And you'll need one, because your employers are *definitely* going to jail tonight," I said.

"I'd appreciate that," Cap'n Bob said, touching the brim of his hat thankfully.

"Can we drop ye off somewhere, chum?" Angus called out to the captain. He was hanging out the window of the driver's seat in one of the dump trucks.

I looked at Cap'n Bob and he nodded.

"Thanks," he said.

"No, thank you," I said. Then I yelled out to everyone left standing around. "Let's get going! Cops will be here in a few minutes. You all know where we're going."

Then I walked over to Ollie, put my arm in his, and we climbed into Angus's truck together.

Minutes later, a line of construction vehicles exited the back gate of the Brasko estate and drove toward the dozens of police vehicles that were responding to a 911 call.

None of the responders had any idea that in the back of the construction trucks were dozens of exotic animals.

Entry Thirty-Six

The tiger paraded himself in front of us, roaring loudly every few minutes just to remind us that he was king of this jungle.

"I can't believe that we got him out just a few days ago," Ollie said, draping himself over one of several fences that stood between us and the big cat. "Doesn't it feel like a lifetime?"

I raised an eyebrow. To me, it felt like just yesterday. But that was probably because as soon as we'd delivered the exotics to Born to Be Wild, everything inside me was finally able to relax.

And boy, had I.

For about forty-eight hours to be exact.

I'd woken up a few times to use the bathroom, but other than that, I'd just slept. Uncle Scotty had assumed I was just being a moody kid and in lieu of having to come up with a credible lie for him, I hadn't corrected him.

When I'd finally emerged, still groggy and starved, Uncle Scotty had told me that Ollie had been by the house twice, and that if he "had to play interference for you again, it might end with Ollie in handcuffs."

"The kid just talks so much," Uncle Scotty had said, looking exhausted himself. "I can't keep up. And he references all this celebrity stuff—it makes my brain want to explode. He's a good kid and I'm glad you have a friend, but couldn't he be a little more like . . . you?"

I'd chuckled.

"Now, do you really want another me running around here?" I'd asked as I poured myself a cup of coffee.

"Right," Uncle Scotty had said, changing his mind.

Now, standing next to Ollie in front of the once-empty tiger enclosure at Born to Be Wild, I'd never want him to be like anyone else.

"I still can't believe we pulled it off," he said with amazement.

"I know," I said. "I think this was the toughest job I've ever done."

"Look at us," Ollie said, jostling me with his elbow. "We're practically pros now!"

"I'm a pro. You're my pro-tégé," I said with authority.

Ollie thought about this for two seconds and then nodded. "I'll take it!"

I laughed.

"Good," I said. "Because I got you something."

"Yay!" Ollie said excitedly, and held out his hand to me.

I promptly slapped it.

"I got you private lessons with a voice coach," I said, smiling at him.

His face fell. "There's nothing to open?" he asked, deflated.

"Come on, this is so much better!" I said. "And it will help you be a better thief. And a better actor. He's going to teach you how to do believable accents."

"I can *do* accents," Ollie said, and started to do what I thought was supposed to be a British accent, but turned out more Australian.

I looked at him blankly.

"No, you can't," I said. When I saw his sad face, I perked up. "But you'll be able to when you're finished with your lessons! And you're a great thief in other ways. You handled the whole Cap'n Bob fiasco beautifully. And that's not something that can be taught. That's just raw talent. Remember, even Angus thought so."

Ollie lifted his chin in the air proudly.

"That's right," he said, starting to smile. "I *am* pretty awesome, aren't I?"

"Oh, geez," I said, worried he was starting to get a big head. "Okay, switching gears now."

"All right," Ollie complied. "How about we talk about what happened between you and Angus the other night."

"What are you talking about?" I asked.

Ollie kicked the fence lightly and looked back up at the tiger we'd saved. I could tell he was avoiding my gaze and I appreciated it.

"Well, I know that Angus offered for you to go with

him when he left. Is it safe to assume you said no since you're still here?" he asked, sounding hopeful.

"Yes," I said, noting how his face lit up as I said the words. "I told him I wanted to stay here."

Ollie tried not to seem overly happy. And I ignored the fact that he was failing miserably at it.

The truth was, I was happy about it too.

With that said, I didn't offer up all of the details of my conversation with my former Scottish co-thief the night of the heist. Including that it had been a tough decision on my part to stay—even if it *was* the right choice for me.

"This was a bit of fun, lass," Angus had said after we'd unloaded all the animals from the construction trucks just outside the sanctuary that night. "I love your spirit. I'd love it even more on the road with me."

He said it like he meant it, and I seriously considered it.

It'd be great to be out there again. I could travel, be a little more like my old self. With Angus as a partner, I wouldn't have to be the mastermind behind our jobs anymore. I wouldn't have the weight of each heist on my shoulders. I could just take my cues from Angus and do my thing.

But was that what I really wanted?

To my surprise, I was actually sort of enjoying being in charge for once. And there was someone else looking up to me and wanting my opinion on things. It was a great feeling, being the master of one's own universe.

And the biggest perk of staying here in Greenwich? I got to choose our jobs. Which meant I could help others. Make the world a better place. As a thief, I'd always assumed to be good, you had to be selfish. Since coming here, I'd discovered that being selfless could sometimes yield greater rewards. For me and for the world.

And I was kind of digging that.

"Sorry, Angus," I had said, giving him a hug. "But I think I'm gonna stick around here a little bit longer. But you'll keep in touch?"

Angus had squeezed me back.

"Of course, lass," he said. "And the offer *always* stands."

I'd slid my hand into the hidden pocket of my catsuit and pulled out the emerald I'd rescued from the snake cage. Then, without thinking too hard about what I was doing, I'd handed it to him.

"Your cut of the job," I'd said, placing the enormous jewel in the palm of his hand.

Angus's eyes grew wide as he held the gem closer to examine it.

"Lass, do ye know what this is worth—"

"A lot, I know," I finished, not wanting to admit out loud just how much I was giving away. "But the truth is, as talented as Ollie is, he couldn't have gotten the job done without your help. You deserve to be compensated for that."

Angus looked at the emerald again and shook his head.

"What would you have done with this if you weren't giving it to me?" he'd asked.

I hadn't had to think about it.

"I'm giving most of our haul to the rescue for taking on all the exotics and for the care they're giving their existing animals," I'd answered. "They do such a great job, but with all of the newbies, they're going to need to expand and that will take money. So . . ."

I'd let the sentence trail off and shrugged.

Angus had studied my face a second.

"You have changed, lass," he'd said quietly, then cut me off as I'd begun to object. "I like it. You're becoming the kind of thief yer mom would've been proud of."

I'd been taken aback by the comment and felt tears start to spring to my eyes.

"Here," Angus had said then, surprising me as he'd handed me back the jewel. "I'm going to take a page out of yer book and give this back to ye. Why dontcha give it to the animals, too."

My eyes had teared up even more and threatened to overflow.

"Are you sure?" I'd asked him.

Angus nodded. "Green's not really my color, anyway."

I'd hugged him again before he'd gotten in his car and headed out of town, on to whatever his next job was.

As I'd watched him drive away, I felt a part of the old me leave, too.

"Yep, looks like you're stuck with me a little longer," I said to Ollie now as we watched another of the tigers we'd rescued come into sight and head over to its old cage-mate.

"You say that like it's a bad thing," Ollie answered. Then, all of a sudden he jumped and turned to face me, an excited look on his face. "Oooh, ooh! I totally forgot to tell you! Adam, the TV crew guy that I made friends with, he texted 'André' yesterday and said that when they got back to the Brasko estate to recover all their gear after the place was raided, they found one of the microphones in the hallway. It had mysteriously been turned on at some point and they'd picked up an interesting conversation between Brigeet and Emma where the heiress confesses everything. You know, before 'Brigeet' disappeared and all."

"Oh, did they now?" I asked, a smile crossing my face.

"Yeah," Ollie said, evaluating my reaction. "He said that the director has decided to go in a different direction with the show. Instead of doing a reality show—which they couldn't finish now anyway—they're going to switch to a docuseries that will follow the attempted rise and fall of one of the US's richest and most powerful families. They say the confession is just the beginning and they'll be filming the investigation and trial now. The twins have already agreed for some bizarre reason.

276

Apparently, they think it could actually make them look *better* to the public?"

"Good luck with that," I muttered. "No way people will be on their side once they hear what she said to me when she thought nobody else was listening. The public is going to burn them at the stake."

"Speaking of *your* part in this," Ollie added, with a silly grin. "Adam asked if I thought Brigeet would go on camera for the doc and talk about her experience facing off with Emma."

I snorted.

"Yeah, no," I said bluntly. "*That's* not happening. I already crossed the line by letting myself be audiotaped."

"So, why'd you do it then?" Ollie asked me.

"I weighed the pros and cons, and ultimately it was more important to get the truth out about what the twins were doing than worry about getting caught."

"Figured you'd say no," Ollie said, looking smug. "So I already told Adam you'd gone back to France and had no plans to come back. And then I threw my phone away."

I tilted my head to the side and placed my hand over my heart. "My little boy is all grown up!" I said with fake emotion.

"Oh, shut up," he said, but I could tell he was happy.

"You guys! I'm surprised to see you back so soon!" a voice called out energetically from behind us. We turned to see Michaela bounding up, her geeky perkiness rolling off her. "Do you have more questions for me or did I succeed in blowing your minds with my entertaining tour the other day?"

"You blew our minds, of course!" Ollie exclaimed, making hand motions like his brain was blowing up.

"But we did want to ask you a few more questions," I chimed in.

"Of course! That's what I'm here for," Michaela said chipperly. "Now, is this about the peculiar shipment we got the other night? Because I've been dying to talk to somebody about it."

"What shipment?" I asked, believably clueless.

Michaela's face lit up.

"Oh, you are in for a treat!" she said to me. Then she looked around to see if anyone else was paying attention and then waved for us to follow her.

We did as she requested, and were brought through a door that read EMPLOYEES ONLY. I caught Ollie's eye as Michaela began to give us a behind-the-scenes look at a section of the rescue we hadn't seen before. Back here, it wasn't quite as polished, but it was clean and stocked.

"So, a few nights ago, I was called into work in the middle of the night because some randos had dropped off over a dozen cages of exotic animals right in front of the rescue's gate!" Michaela said.

"You're kidding!" I said.

Michaela nodded. "It's true!" she exclaimed like I really needed convincing. "There were, like, ten tigers, a sloth, some monkeys, a few others."

"Where'd they come from?" I asked.

Michaela bit at her thumbnail. "I don't know. But thank gosh they did, because some of the animals were in bad shape."

"They were?" Ollie asked, surprised to hear it.

"Yeah," she said. "Some were malnourished, others had old injuries that hadn't been addressed. There were a few that were simply scared to death."

"And now?" I asked her.

"And now, they're safe because they're here," she said, waving her hand at the group of oversized cages now in front of us that held many of the animals we'd freed. "We even got some baby cubs! Aren't they cute? Don't get too close, though. They're still deadly, even if you wish you could squeeze their little faces off!"

"Cute," I said, remembering how they'd stalked me that night in the Jungle Room.

"But that's not the craziest part," Michaela said, lowering her voice to a near-whisper. Ollie and I moved closer to indulge her. "Yesterday we got an anonymous donation sent to the sanctuary. And it was a *lot*.

"Whoa!" Ollie said.

"That's nuts!" I echoed, playing our part in the little show.

"Now, I don't know exactly how much was there . . . ," Michaela said, her eyes wide now.

Five hundred thousand dollars.

". . . but the rumor is, it was enough to do a whole

new addition to the rescue and run things for the next decade. Can you believe it?" she finished finally.

"That's amazing," I said to her, and smiled.

My cell phone buzzed in my pocket and I took it out to glance at the text.

Uncle Scotty: **Meet me at The Farm in 20?**

I moved my fingers quickly over the screen, letting Ollie and Michaela carry on their conversation without me.

Me: **Sure. See you soon.**

"Sorry guys, duty calls," I said, holding up my phone. "Gotta get going. Michaela, now that you've got so many more animals to take care of, you guys probably need more help, huh?"

Michaela blinked at me.

"Yeah. Actually, Jolene, the owner was just mentioning that this morning," she said, curiously. "Why? Are you offering?"

I chuckled at her joke. "I think I know someone who would be perfect. Can I put you guys in touch?"

"Could they start now? As you can see, we're sort of overwhelmed around here," she said.

"Yeah," I said, smiling. "I think he could make himself available."

Entry Thirty-Seven

I had no idea why Uncle Scotty wanted me to meet him.

The even bigger head-scratcher was that he wanted to do it at The Farm.

So, I was a bit in the dark—and on edge—when I walked up to Kayla's shop. I stopped just outside, pausing for a minute before I walked in.

As I looked around, gathering myself, my eyes fell on a long, thin stick lying just a few feet away. Smiling, I bounced over and picked it up, running my hand along its rough, scratchy surface.

Then I went back to the front door and pushed it open as slowly as I could. I watched the crack at the top open an inch. Then two. Two and a half, and I finally saw it.

I deftly lifted the branch and stuck it up into the area between the bell and where it was attached above the door. I grinned and opened the door the rest of the way, noting with satisfaction how it made zero noise.

Victory!

I slowly closed the door again and leaned the branch up against the wall before walking farther into the store.

I was so sick of hearing that darn bell ring every time I walked inside.

I didn't see Uncle Scotty or Kayla, so I headed toward the back, listening for their voices as I went. When I arrived in the inner sanctum, the only ones there were the animals currently waiting for a forever home.

"Hi everyone!" I said.

They all seemed to perk up and a few even started to bark back.

This is how I should be greeted all the time.

Something snagged on my T-shirt as I walked toward the back door and I turned to look at what it was.

"Geronimo!" I said, reaching up and gently retracting the animal's claws from the material of my shirt. "I see you, girl."

I picked the cat up and nuzzled my face into her fluffy fur.

"You're much better behaved than those big cats," I said, petting her lovingly. "Should we go find Uncle Scotty?"

I took her meow as a yes and walked out the back door of The Farm. As we emerged into the back parking lot, I spotted Uncle Scotty and Kayla about fifty feet away. They were huddled together in the cold and talking quietly to each other.

I kept my footsteps silent and moved carefully toward them. Geronimo did her part and kept quiet too, as if she knew what we were doing. When we were just a few feet away, I finally caught parts of their conversation.

"There would be four main yards, each with a different

theme and gear," Kayla was saying. "We'll set up shades, water misters in the summer, space heaters in the winter. A swimming pool, pup pads, toys, cushy fake grass— Ahhhh! I'm just so excited!"

"What are we excited about?" I asked as I let my presence be known.

Kayla jumped while Uncle Scotty turned to look at me, an eyebrow raised questioningly.

"Frankie!" Kayla exclaimed in her soft, sing-songy voice. "You're here!"

"Yep," I said, carefully. "Uncle Scotty asked me to come?"

"Oh, right," she said, exchanging a look with my uncle that I didn't quite understand.

We all stood there silently, just looking at each other and not speaking. Finally, I cleared my throat and spoke up.

"Okay," I said, confused. "So, we're excited, why?"

Kayla's face lit up again and she nearly jumped up and down in delight.

"You won't believe this, but The Farm has a fairy godmother!" Kayla said, her eyes wide.

"A fairy godmother?" I asked, thoroughly confused. I looked over at Uncle Scotty for some sort of explanation and he just shrugged before gesturing back at the rescue owner.

"There's no other explanation than that," Kayla said. "Yesterday I came to the barn and found an envelope addressed to me. When I opened it, I found a bunch of money and a note saying I should use it to build the animal yard! Can you believe it?"

I put the appropriate look of shock and amazement on my face.

"That's amazing!" I said, shaking my head. "Well, if anyone deserves it, it's you and this place."

"It's just—what an incredible gift," she said, looking so grateful.

"I bet whoever gave the money to you felt like you're the incredible one," I said, petting Geronimo. "You take care of all these guys when no one else will and you try to find them families. You're like an animal superhero."

Kayla blushed.

"I'm just trying to make the world a little better," she said finally. "Isn't that what most people are striving for? Leaving the world a little better because they were here?"

"Not everyone is as altruistic as you," Uncle Scotty said seriously. "Case in point, the reason I'm here."

"Right," Kayla said, frowning. "Well, that's why we need more people like my fairy godmother."

"Why *are* you here?" I asked Uncle Scotty, still confused by that fact.

Uncle Scotty took a breath.

"A few days ago there was a raid at the estate of a couple local billionaires," Uncle Scotty said, placing his hands into the pockets of his jeans. "When we responded to a call from someone in the house, we found a twelve-foot snake and a bunch of empty cages. After an investigation we discovered that the owners have been running an illegal exotic trade business, capturing and supplying endangered animals to others across the US."

"Geez," I said. "Some people really suck."

"They do suck," my uncle said without thinking. When he saw Kayla and my faces at his response, he straightened up, looking embarrassed. "Anyways, I'm here because I was asking Kayla if she'd take the snake we confiscated."

"And I politely declined and gave your uncle the name of the organization that just took in the boa we had here the other day," Kayla said. "I'm not qualified to handle a snake that size."

"Yeah, that's no joke," I said before I could stop myself. "I mean, you said it was twelve feet long? At that size, I'd imagine it could eat . . . well, Geronimo here. Can't have that."

"That's right," Kayla said slowly, still studying me. After a few seconds, she looked from Uncle Scotty and back to me. "Okay, I'll let you guys talk."

Then she did the strangest thing. She gave my uncle a wink before walking away.

What the heck was *that* about?

"We need to talk?" I asked Uncle Scotty curiously once Kayla had disappeared inside.

Uncle Scotty turned to me, a slightly uncomfortable look on his face.

Uh-oh.

"I've been chatting with Kayla on and off since you expressed how much you and Ollie get along with her," Uncle Scotty started. He began to pace around the parking lot. "And there was something I wanted to talk to you about. Well, *we* wanted to talk to you about."

We?

What. Is. Going. On?

"Okay . . . ," I said carefully.

"Well, as we were talking, Kayla told me that she'd asked if you wanted to adopt a cat?" he said, scratching his chin.

I held the cat up and waved her paw at him.

"Meet Geronimo," I said.

"Hello," he said awkwardly, before getting back to his point. "She said you said no, because you 'weren't a cat person'? Is that true?"

I shrugged. I realized it was unfortunate timing as I was currently cuddling with said cat.

"It's more like I'm not really a *pet* person. Besides, you said I couldn't bring any animals home."

There, that should do it.

Uncle Scotty stopped pacing and looked at me. "Maybe I was wrong."

Huh?

"Huh?" I asked. "What are you talking about?"

"Maybe a pet is *just* what we need," he said cautiously.

I gave him a weird look.

He held up his hands in front of him. "Now hear me out," he said. "So, the other day, we were talking about change and how we can only grow as much as we're willing to change. I think you—deep down—don't think you're a pet person, because *you've never had the opportunity to have a pet.*"

Did he read my journal or my mind? He couldn't be that dead-on just on his own. I didn't give him enough of my inner thoughts to let him read me like that.

Then again, I was talking to a detective.

I began to open my mouth to argue with him but he stopped me.

"Now, I could be way off base here, but from what Kayla says and what I'm seeing now, you don't *dislike* animals. And if that's true, then I'm inclined to believe that you don't want a pet because you still don't see this as your home. You don't want to lay down roots."

I didn't confirm whether he was right, but also didn't deny it. So, he continued.

"That got me thinking—maybe we *both* need to change a little bit to become even better versions of ourselves," he said. "So, I wanted to challenge you to change the way you feel about being here, in Greenwich. Instead of feeling like you're *stuck* here forever, how about you look at this as the home you can always *go back* to after your adventures. It will be your home whenever you want it. But for that to be true, you have to start doing things that ground you here."

"Like bringing home a pet?" I asked, stroking Geronimo as she purred.

"Like bringing home a pet," he agreed.

"Well, what are you changing about yourself?" I asked, curious to know what flaws he felt he had.

"I think that by us bringing home this cat, it will force me to stop thinking that I'm incapable of taking care of somebody else," he said, sounding a little embarrassed to admit it. "Namely, you."

"I'm not a plant, Uncle Scotty," I said, jokingly. "I can remember to water myself."

Uncle Scotty laughed, but I could tell he'd meant what he'd said.

"Thank gosh," he said, faking relief. Then his smile faded. "But on a serious note, I do worry about whether I'm doing a good job being . . . parenty. Am I the best person to be raising a young girl? Am I enough for you? Am I doing everything wrong despite trying to do everything right? It's hard for me to . . . be the sole person someone relies on to stay alive."

"I get that," I said, thinking about my little meltdown after realizing I'd put Ollie in danger with the exotics.

"So, maybe we take this cat home, and I can work on my fear of bringing home strays, and you can work on staying put for a while and not feeling so fenced in. What do you say?"

I lowered my head and breathed in Geronimo's smell.

She was perfect. Not too needy but there when you did need her.

And I'd loved her at first sight, which rarely happened with me. I hadn't even liked Ollie the first time I'd met him.

"Okay," I agreed. "But I'm not cleaning up her poop."

Uncle Scotty came over and hugged me and Geronimo at the same time.

"Geronimo is both of our responsibilities. We'll *both* be cleaning her poop," he said, then made a face.

"Fiiiiine," I said, acting annoyed. Then I held my new pet's squishy face up to mine and said, "What do you say, girl? Wanna come home with us? We're all kinds of crazy, but you'll be loved."

Then I started to laugh.

It was the perfect description of what you got when you entered a Lordes' house.

ACKNOWLEDGMENTS

I'd like to thank everyone who had a hand in making this book happen.

That means you.

Yeah, you, there in the back.

I absolutely *couldn't* have finished *Going Wild* without *your* help and support.

Also, **Bethany Buck**, my editor extraordinaire. Thank you for loving Frankie like I do and for watching my back along the way.

The ultra-talented folks at Pixel+Ink, who took my words and shaped them into the book you're reading now. So much love to Sara DiSalvo, Michelle Montague, Terry Borzumato-Greenberg, Steve Scott, Whitney Fine, Raina Putter, Lisa Lee, Hannah Finne, Julia Gallagher, Miriam Miller, Alison Weiss, Mary Cash, and Derek Stordahl.

Reiko Davis, you've become more than just an agent to me. You're my sounding board, my cheerleader, and most of all, my friend. Thank you for your confidence, advice, and kindness. You're rad.

La-la-la-la-la-la-la, a little bit **Kayla**. Thanks for lending me your ear, opinions, and name to the second installation of Frankie.

Natasha, I appreciate all the texts of encouragement and check-ins you sent while I was writing this book. Thank you for being willing to read version one of *Going Wild*. You're an author's dream reader. And a gal's best friend.

Mom, I know that I've created a great book when you can't wait to read the next chapter. I couldn't ask for a better compliment or support system.

Dad, you're not an infamous international thief, but you *have* taught me a thing or two over the years. Thanks for fueling my love of creativity and talking books with me.

Jacey, you are the basis for every cool character I've ever written.

Amy, you always challenge me to be better.

Andrea and **Price**, nobody has more fantastic in-laws than I do. Nobody. Well, except for maybe Katy.

Katy, your dedication, determination, and drive inspire me. You're more than a SIL.

Ryan, your accomplishments keep me on my toes. Your support is boundless.